Thomas Edward Bartlett

The Bartletts

Ancestral, Genealogical, Biographical, Historical

Thomas Edward Bartlett

The Bartletts
Ancestral, Genealogical, Biographical, Historical

ISBN/EAN: 9783337074760

Printed in Europe, USA, Canada, Australia, Japan

Cover: Foto ©Raphael Reischuk / pixelio.de

More available books at **www.hansebooks.com**

THE BARTLETTS.

Ancestral, Genealogical, Biographical,

Historical.

COMPRISING AN ACCOUNT OF THE

AMERICAN PROGENITORS OF THE BARTLETT
FAMILY, WITH SPECIAL REFERENCE
TO THE DESCENDANTS OF

JOHN BARTLETT,

OF

WEYMOUTH AND CUMBERLAND.

BY

THOMAS EDWARD BARTLETT

NEW HAVEN, CONN.
PRESS OF THE STAFFORD PRINTING CO., 86-90 CROWN STREET.
1892.

" Happy who, with bright regard looks back
  Upon his father's fathers ; who with joy
  Recounts their deeds of grace, and in himself
  Values the latest link in the fair chain
  Of noble sequences ; for nature loves
  Not at one bound to achieve her topmost type,
  But step by step she leads a family on
  To demigod or devil ; the rare joy
  Or horror of the world."

—*Goethe's Iphigenia.*

(Bani[5]; Eber[4]; Joseph[3]; Jacob[2]; John[1]).

MEMORIAL.

T HIS work, the imperfect result of much loving labor, was
inspired by grateful remembrance of the tender, patient,
noble-minded Eber Bartlett, father of the Author and Compiler. It is very likely, an unimportant tribute to a man
whose unselfish life was very rich in benefit to his children
and all others, even of alien households, but there is a com-
fort of a peculiar kind, founded upon most grateful recollections of one of the kindest of parents, in thus dedicating to him
the result of very many days pleasantly and perhaps not quite
unprofitably, occupied. With reverential affection has the
writer ever borne in mind the gentle, courageous, forbearing
ancestor, whose virtues are herein altogether too indifferently
commemorated.

BARTLETT NAME.

Of names distinguished in the colonial town and state annals of our American Union, none is of more uniformly honorable record than that of Bartlett. The name frequently appears in connection with momentous events of New England's early days, the actors in which will be remembered for the greatness of their deeds, the strength of their patriotism, and for the tenacity of their adherence to principle. Some who have borne the name, while not perhaps eminent for the splendor of their public career, are properly entitled to grateful remembrance for their exemplary conduct and successful endeavor in good citizenship, and as friends of their fellow men.

Many of the immediate descendants of John Bartlett of Weymouth and Cumberland appear to have been Quakers. This society at that early period, required excessive plainness in dress and the utmost simplicity in all the affairs of life. They were opposed to war and were exempted from military duty, and the payment of taxes for war purposes, and their disapproval of office-holding and political controversy, prevented a public recognition of the worth and virtue that was so conspicuously apparent in the lives of many of its members. That so many of the Bartletts—although Quakers—did accept positions of honor and trust in the administration of the government, notwithstanding the incompatibility of their religious

environments, is suggestive of the esteem in which they were
held by their neighbors.

It is impracticable in a work like this, circumscribed in
scope and necessarily brief in details, to trace the Bartlett
lineage since the date when the name first appears in colonial
and plantation archives. The intention of the compiler has
been, simply by patient research and labor, to preserve for the
use of biographers, who, in future, may offer a fuller account of
the Bartletts, an accurate transcript of existing data, gathered
from numerous reliable sources.. The notes from which this
compilation has been made were taken, as opportunity per-
mitted, during a period of some years, and they are placed in a
form to assist any student of the Bartlett records in a com-
prehension of some of the interesting information collected.

The want of continuity and completeness of much of the
documentary matter in the public records of Massachusetts
and Rhode Island, and the defective registration of the earlier
vital statistics, has rendered necessary a long and patient
research. All available advantage has been taken of extant
writings, published histories, biographies, and genealogies, as
found in various public and private libraries. Most of the
information thus obtained has been corroborated by deeds
and wills, found at different places and in other ways It
should not be surprising if here and there an error were discernible or suspected, and indeed the public records in many
instances have not been infallible ; but it is believed that the
important features of this work are well established by suffi-
cient evidence of truth, notwithstanding there should be a
lapse, or mistake, caused by copying, or error in the date of a
birth, or death. No attempt has been made to present a work
of a biographical character, as the voluminous amount accessi-
ble would in itself make a book many times larger than this;
but instead to ascertain whatever was essential as an aid in
connecting the different families of the name during the first
hundred years of the settlement of the Bartletts in this country ; for, at the outset of the labor of compilation, there was
an uncertainty in regard to the headship of families to which
many persons of the name distinguished in widely different
walks of life, belonged.

No small exercise of patience is required to collate facts concerning the separate families of any name, so as to illumine the history of some ancestral founder, and this is peculiarly the case touching the Bartlett families, they having been so numerous at the time of the early settlement of the country. Had there been a less number of collateral progenitors, the labor of compilation would have been less difficult. Some of the problems connected with the history of this branch of the Bartlett family, are satisfactorily settled by the facts now made known in these pages, and thus has been prepared a starting point, from which can be pursued the succession in families, and it is believed that all, who belong to this branch of the Bartletts, can without difficulty find their place upon the family tree. If this book should have the effect to promote and strengthen an interest in whatever is connected with the name of Bartlett, it will not have been uselessly printed. It has been prepared with affectionate remembrance of a loving father whose interest in kindred, unselfish devotion to his family, and adherence to principle, endeared him to his children.

THOMAS EDWARD BARTLETT.

THE ORIGINAL COAT OF ARMS.

THE PRESENT COAT OF ARMS.

THE
BARTLETT ANCESTRY.

All persons in this country, named Bartlett, are without doubt of Norman ancestry. There is a large estate at Stopham, Sussex, England, consisting of some thousands of acres, which has been in possession of the Bartletts for hundreds of years. From junior members of this family in former times, came the first settlers on these American shores. The Ancestral Mansion was built in 1309, and is a noble building of stone. Near it, stands the old Norman Church, built by the family in the Thirteenth century, and on the stone floor, along the aisles of the church, are marble slabs with inset figures of brass, showing a regular succession of Bartletts, from John, who died in 1428, to Colonel George Bartlett, or Barttelot, as the name was spelled in early times, who died in November, 1872, aged 84 years. Here have the Bartletts lived since the time of the Norman invasion. The first of the family was Adam Barttelot, an esquire in the retinue of Brian, a Knight, and they came into England with William, the Conqueror, and fought at Hastings. Both were granted lands. In the Fifteenth century, a castle appears as the crest of the coat of arms which was granted by Edward, the Black Prince, to John Barttelot, for taking the castle of Fontenoy, in France. In the Sixteenth century, a swan was added, and granted, by the Garter King of Arms. Since that time, the crest is double a castle, and swan. The original coat of arms of the family was three open, left-hand, falconer's gloves, with golden tassels about the wrist. The coat of arms now in use is very elaborate, representing different coats of arms of families who have inter-married with the Barttelots. The quarterings of Smith, Musgrave and Boldero, were added in 1875, when Sir Walter B. Barttelot, the present representative of the family, was created a baronet.

The family lineage with the succession from the Norman
ancestor to the present time, may be found in Sir Bernard
Burke's " Genealogical and Heraldic Dictionary of the Peer-
age and Baronetage," which in England is the authoritative
book of titular genealogical reference ; almost every public
library in this country has a copy amongst its standard works
of reference.

The name is spelt in many different ways in the family
record, B-a-r-t-t-e-l-o-t occuring most frequently in the older
documents.   At the present time—with few exceptions—the
spelling is B-a-r-t-l-e-t-t.   It appears that, in former times,
many of the younger members of the family, who were obliged
to seek their fortunes elsewhere on the accession of their elder
brother to the entailed inheritance, adopted a different spelling
of the name.   It is quite evident that this change in spelling
was not, originally, wholly the result of caprice or accident.
The intention may have been that it should be designative,
to denote the diminutive, or lesser, of the Barttelots.   Sir
Walter, like most of his predecessors who were incumbents of
the ancestral estate, uses the ancient Norman orthography.

The origin of the name does not appear to be known.   Its
existence at such a remote period would seem to prevent any
intelligent supposition as to the way it first originated.   The
derivation from Bartholemew, as presented by a writer on sur-
names, appears labored and "far-fetched," and without cor-
roborative reference, will fail to satisfy the enquirer.

JOHN BARTLETT.

OF

WEYMOUTH AND CUMBERLAND.

The earliest record, to this time discovered, concerning the
progenitor of the Weymouth and Cumberland Bartletts, is
found in the town records of Weymouth, Mass. There is only
one entry. It reads :

> "John Bartlett, son of John Bartlett and Sarah his wife.
> Born February 11, 1666."

Whence came the father of the boy whose birth is recorded,
or in what relationship he stood to the others of similar sur-
name, then living in this country, future enquiry may reveal.

In order to more clearly understand the conditions, and surroundings, of the subject of this sketch, and his descendants at
that early period and to prevent confusion in fixing the places
where they located, it appears convenient to mention in proper
connection, as nearly as possible, some of the leading features
of the incorporation, and settlement, of the towns in which
they resided, and with the history of the foundation of which,
they are identified.

As new towns were frequently set off and divided from the older ones,
the personages herein mentioned will appear as residents of different towns,
although their location was not changed.

We learn from the historian, that in 1622, Thomas Weston,
a wealthy merchant of London, who had been interested in
the Plymouth Colony, procured a patent for a tract of land
on Massachusetts bay and immediately fitted out at his own
expense two ships with fifty or sixty men each, for the purpose of settling a plantation. On arrival at Plymouth, many
of them being sick, they remained there most of the summer
and were treated, it is said, with great kindness by the inhabi-

tants.   While convalescing, frequent excursions were made by the more able of the company into the adjacent country, for the purpose of finding a suitable place for settlement. They finally concluded to occupy a place on Massachusetts bay, named by the Indians, Wessagusett, and early in the fall the entire company removed thither and started a plantation.

The company proved, however, to be disorderly, many of them being, as reported, "profane and badly governed," and by their extravagance the colony became reduced to want, thereby causing much suffering. In their intercourse with the Indians they had incurred their enmity by taking their corn and otherwise ill-treating them, and but for the timely assistance of the famous Captain Miles Standish and his little company from Plymouth, they would undoubtedly have been destroyed. The danger being so great from the continued hostilities of the natives, it was deemed advisable to abandon the plantation, and this was accordingly done.

This disastrous termination of the settlement was unfortunate, as Mr. Weston's designs were said to be philanthropic and but for the mismanagement, of his agents, would have proved successful.

Mr. Weston, who was in London, on being informed of the condition of things in the colony, started at once for the scene of disorder and lost his life while trying to reach the coast.[*]

It appears there were a few inhabitants there in 1624, but whether they were of the original party, is not known. It is stated that at this time, 1624, "The few inhabitants of Wessagussett received an accession to their number," among the arrivals being Captain Robert Gorges (Georges) and Rev. William Morrill, from Weymouth, England, and the place is supposed to have been called "Weymouth" after this date.[†]

The town was incorporated September 2, 1635, and the same year, Mr. Hull, a minister from England, and twenty-one families joined the settlement. This town, with many others, suffered during King Phillip's war, and there were seven or eight houses burned by the Indians.

[*] The various versions by different writers touching Mr. Weston's motives in settling the plantation, and the time and manner of his death, is not important in this connection.

[†] Next to Plymouth, it was the earliest settled town in the State.

Some time after the birth of their eldest son, John Bartlett and his wife appear to have removed from Weymouth to Mendon, Mass. The latter place had already been settled by people from Weymouth and Braintree and was, probably, incorporated as a town before his arrival.

Mendon, next to Lancaster, is the oldest town in Worcester County and at that time was not the contracted town of to-day, but included a part of Bellingham, all of Milford and Blackstone, a large part of Upton and Northbridge and all Uxbridge.

Bellingham was incorporated as a town November 27, 1719, from parts of Mendon, Dedham and Wrentham.

Milford [the Indian name was "Wopowage,"] was incorporated April 11, 1780, from the east precinct of Mendon.

Blackstone was incorporated March 25, 1845, from Mendon.

Upton was incorporated June 14, 1735, from a part of Mendon, Sutton, Uxbridge, and Hopkinton.

Northbridge was incorporated July 14, 1772, from the north part of Uxbridge; parts of Sutton were annexed February 17, 1801, and March 16, 1844.

Uxbridge (Indian name, "Waeuntug,") was incorporated June 27, 1727, from Mendon. The original grant for Mendon was for eight miles square, but the grantees took possession of nearly double that extent of territory. At a General Court holden in Boston, October 16, 1660, "in further answer to Braintry's petition, the Court declare they judge meete and proper to grant a plantation of eight miles square and that the persons named have liberty to enter upon and make a beginning thereat."

This tract was purchased from the Indians for "twenty-four pound sterling," and a deed was given "Anawassanauk alias John Quashoamait alias William, of Blue Hills; Great John Namsconont alias Peter, and Upannbohqueen alias Jacob of Natic," to Moses Payne and Peter Brackett, "both of Brantre." The deed was dated April 22, 1662, and witnessed by John Elliot, Sr., John Elliot, Jr., and Daniel Weld, Sr. At the time of the above grant the Court ordered "that Major Atherton, Lieut. Roger Clapp, Elezur Lusher and Deacon Parke, or any three of them, shall be and are hereby empowered to make a valid act there." These were denominated the Committee of Nipmug, which was the original name of the town.

This was the Country of the Nipmug (sometimes called Nipnet and Nipmuck), Indians whose headquarters was said to have been at what is now Oxford, Mass. October 30, 1663, this committee ordered that all persons who had accepted allotments of land in the plantation should remove there with their families by the middle of November, 1664, "upon penaltie of forfeiture of all the grants there."

The first settlers from Braintree were, John Moore, George Aldrich, Daniel Lovett, Josiah Chapin, Ferdinando Thayer, John Scammell, Nathaniel Haseman, Alexander Plumley, Matthias Puller, John Woodland, John Hasber, Joseph Penniman and John Gurney. Those from Weymouth were, Goodman King, Sr., Walter Cook, William Holbrook, Joseph White, Goodman Thomson, Goodman John Raynes, Goodman Bolter, Sr., Abraham

Staples, Samuel Pratt and Thomas Boller, all of which had land allotted them prior to their removal to the town.

At a General Court held in Boston, May 15, 1667, the plantation of Nipmug, now called Quinshepauge, was incorporated by the name of Mendon, taking its name probably from the town of Mendham, County of Suffolk, England. Mendon was attached to the County of Middlesex, May 12, 1670.

The original inhabitants settled in what is now called the North Parish. Matthias Puffer erected the second mill in 1681, near where the first one stood, which belonged to Benjamin Albee. Sergeant Josiah Chapin built the first saw mill. It was on Muddy Brook, some distance above where the present road to Milford crosses it. Joseph and Angell Torry, soon after, built a saw mill on School Brook, near where Obadiah Wood's and Lyman Keith's mill stands. Joseph Stevens was the first blacksmith and James Bick the second.

At a town meeting, October 22, 1730, it was voted to provide "a Barrel of Rhum" toward the raising of the new meeting house.

According to Metcalf's "Annals of Mendon," John Bartlett was supposed to be the contractor for building the minister's (Grindal Rawson) house. For it was voted, November 14, 1681, that a note for £16 "deu to John Bartlett should be made to be paid; the one half in Indian corn, att two shillings a bushel and the other half in pork att 2 pence a pound," this being the same that was to be paid when the house was finished.

The first appearance of the name of John Bartlett upon the Mendon records is as follows: "At a town meeting held January 1, 1671-2, their was granted to John Bartlett a twenty Acor house lotte with all the rights and privileges that other 20 acor lottes have only this accepted that he stay for his Meadow untill all ye inhabitants that came before be satisfied."

At a town meeting, March 18, 1671-2, "It was voted and granted that John Bartlett shall pay £10 for his lot and take it up by the side of the Mill land." The location of this lot which was soon after laid out to him is described as being on the "west side of Mill river, just above the mill pond, and butted and bounded as followeth: Butted northerly upon Common land with a line of marked trees and stakes. Bounded southerly upon Common land with a line of marked trees and stakes. Westerly, partly upon the land of John Dike and partly upon the land of Albee*, and easterly upon Common

---

*Probably Benjamin Albee, who built the first grist mill in Mendon, at this place. It was destroyed by Indians 1675. It was situated near where Nathan Allen's mill now stands. The house lot which was laid out here to John Bartlett, can thus be readily located by any one who so desires. The record shows that John sold his house lot April 3, 1679, but to whom it is not stated.

land with a line of marked trees and stakes with a by-way of ten rod wide running through the sd land, the whole sum being twenty acors more or less."

The next month, April 14, 1671-2, at a drawing for meadow, John drew lot No. 9, which was situated "below Meadfield road on the Mill Plain and on the edge of 2nd bridges* plain," and " on both sides of Beaver pond brook," and also on the "north side of Charles river," and was on the east side of Caleb's hill.†

The birth of two of the children of John Bartlett and his wife Sarah are recorded in Mendon, viz : Mary, born January 1, 1679, and Noah, born January 29, 1680. The others, with the exception of Daniel, who was born January 24, 1684, and recorded in Rehoboth, were probably all born between the time of the birth of the eldest son, John, Jr., at Weymouth in 1666, and Mary, born in Mendon, 1679, but no record of their birth has been discovered. Neither is it known where they resided during the Indian troubles, or the time of King Phillip's war, from 1675 to 1680, which caused the desolation of the town of Mendon. It is presumed, however, that they went with the others who are said to have returned to Weymouth and Braintree ; although it is possible they may have gone to the island of Rhode Island, where many of the settlers sought refuge during that eventful period.

The last entry in the Mendon records, before the burning of the town by the Indians, was a record of transactions at a town meeting holden May 6, 1675. The next town meeting, after the close of the war and the return of the inhabitants, was held January 3, 1680. During this interval of about five years, there was no entry made on the town books.

This war, commonly called " King Phillip's War," which desolated the country for several years and came near driving the white settlers from New England, is spoken of in Hubbard's Narrative as follows :

" On the 24th of June, 1675, was the alarm of war first sounded in Plymouth Colony, where eight or nine were slain in and about Swansea." By the same authority we are told that the first blood spilled in the Massachusetts Colony, was at Mendon.

In 1671, a son of Matoonus, one of the Nipmuck, or Nipnett Indians, had been executed at Worcester settlement, for the murder of an Englishman,

*2nd bridges was the name for one of the branches of Charles River.
†This was in what is now Milford.

and his head was placed on a pole, where it remained a long time, a
ghastly warning to evil-doers. The father, a grave and sober Indian, who
had been constable of Pakachoag by Gookin, although professing Christian-
ity, had no doubt been brooding over the death of his offspring, and with
the vindictive principles, so deeply cherished by his people, had only
waited for an opportunity to revenge himself. This he did by making a raid
on the defenseless settlers at Mendon, July 10, 1675, which resulted in the
killing of five of the inhabitants. It is related in John W. Barber's Historical Collections that Richard Post, according to tradition, was the first
victim, and was killed near where the office of William Hastings stood.
Post lived on the road leading from Mendon to Sherburn, now discontinued
as a highway, but still called " Post's Lane."

John Bartlett, then of Mendon, June 6, 1682, bought of
William Sabin, fifty acres of land on the Pawtucket River, now
called the Blackstone River, in Rehoboth, at a place called by
the Indians, "Shunasetaconet," and described in the deed as
lying "between the ancient bounds of Rehoboth and the line
between the governments." This deed was recorded in the
Cumberland records in 1748, nearly sixty-seven years afterward.

The ancient boundary of Rehoboth was the Pawtucket River, which
divided it from Providence on the west, and Massachusetts Colony on the
north. Rehoboth was first called Seacunck, or Seakonk, and was granted
to people of Hingham and purchased of the Indian chief, Massasoit, in 1641,
but the real settlement did not probably commence until 1643, when Rev.
Samuel Newman moved there with the majority of his church, from Wey-
month. The first meeting of the original planters on record is dated at
" Weimouth, the 24th of the 8th month, 1643." The first tract was called
eight miles square, but at the present day it would easily measure ten. The
old-fashioned method of defining boundaries by an occasional perambula-
tion by town officers was advantageous to the settlers. It is not to be supposed that these pious functionaries intended to cheat the Indians, but the
acres were of liberal size as measured by them.
The first addition to the territory of the town was made in 1645, when that
tract of land called Wannamoiset, which joined the original grant on the
south and which included what is now a part of Swansey, Barrington, and
Warren, R. I., was purchased and annexed. The next purchase and grant,
and also the last one, was called the North Purchase, and was made in
1661, of Wamsitta, then Sachem of Pokanoket,* and comprised that territory which was afterward Attleboro and Cumberland, R. I. Attleboro
was set off from Rehoboth and incorporated October 19th, 1694, and
comprised the present town and Cumberland.† That part of Attleboro,
since of Cumberland, was called the "Gore," and later, "Cumberland
Gore," and was frequently denominated " that gore of land in controversy
between the governments."‡

*Wamsitta's original name was Mooanam, but was commonly called Alexander. He was
a son of Massasoit and elder brother of King Philip. [Bliss' History of Rehoboth."]
†Woonsocket was taken partly from Cumberland, January 31, 1867.
‡Prior to 1746, the boundary line between Rhode Island and Massachusetts had not been
settled and there had been for many years much feeling manifested in regard to the dispute,
frequent petitions being sent to the mother country, each party claiming more than the other
was willing to concede.

CUMBERLAND INCORPORATED.

The place where many of the descendants of John Bartlett had settled was within the disputed territory and near the line of the present boundary between Rhode Island and Massachusetts. There was great inconvenience in not knowing to what town or state their holdings should be rated. This vexatious question was at last settled, however, and January 27, 1746-7, the gore of land belonging to Attleboro was annexed to Rhode Island and incorporated as the town of Cumberland, its name being taken from Cumberland, England, which it is said to resemble, it being like the latter town, rich in mineral wealth. Old deeds which had remained unrecorded for years, owing to the interested parties not knowing in which town their possessions lay, were then brought forward and duly recorded.

In Arnold's History of Rhode Island, Vol. II., there is a copy of a map which was sent to England during the boundary controversy, which represents the whole territory—the "Gore,"—between Abbot's Run and the Pawtucket River as being "Seneechataconett."[*] It is possible that the whole of that section had become at that late period, known by that name, but from the wording of numerous conveyances, there can be little doubt that at the early time when John Bartlett bought his land and took up his residence there, the name had a local significance and applied directly to this place, now known as Manville, R. I. This appears more probable because there is an island here which was called Seneechetaco-

[*]Shannatt conett, where John Bartlett located in Rehoboth, is, like most Indian names, spelled many different ways, but the spelling here adopted appears to have been the most common. The very diversified orthography, found in the early town records, has been perplexing. It was thought best, when practicable, to reproduce the original, especially when spelling the names of persons.

nett Island. It being also one of the principal fording places and the only one in that vicinity, at that time, it would give the locality that importance which would require a name. Had not this place been called and known by the name of Senechetaconet, the land which John Bartlett here bought of William Sabin would have been described in the deed as "the fording place."

On the west side of the Blackstone River, in what was known as Providence Plantations, several changes took place, which it will be well to mention, as the Bartletts occupied considerable territory of what was afterward Scituate, Smithfield and Gloucester, R. I. The town founded by Roger Williams in 1636 and named Providence, "in gratitude to his Supreme Deliverer," originally included the whole of the north part of the State of Rhode Island west of the Blackstone River, and no division was made until February 20, 1730-1. At this date, an act was passed "for erecting and incorporating the outlands of the town of Providence into three towns." These towns were Scituate, Smithfield and Gloucester. Since that time there have been many sub-divisions. Burrillville, named after Hon. James Burrill, was set off from Gloucester, October 29, 1806, and the town of Lincoln, named in honor of the late Abraham Lincoln, President of the United States, was taken from Smithfield, March 8, 1871. There was also a part of Smithfield appropriated, in connection with that taken from Cumberland in the foundation of the new town of Woonsocket, incorporated January 31, 1867. Other towns were formed and incorporated from the very large tract of land which first comprised the so-called Providence Plantations.

As John Bartlett had removed to Rehoboth, and within the jurisdiction of Plymouth, according to the custom of those times, he was obliged to take the oath of allegiance, or "fidelity," to that government. This he did, as we find the following in the Plymouth Colony Court Records, June 6, 1683:

"This Court, Captain Richmond, of Little Compton, and John Bartlett, of Rehoboth, took the oath of fidelitie to this government."*

John Bartlett and his wife did not long enjoy their new possessions. The Rehoboth records have this: †"John Bartlett buried 17th August, 1684. Sarah, wife of John Bartlett, buried 17th January, 1684-5." After her husband's death,

*Precisely one year from the date of the deed of land which he bought from William Sabin.

†It was the custom at that time, in Rehoboth, to record the date of burial instead of the time of death. This was also the method in a few other towns in early times. The dates are under the O. S. computation or reckoning. By the Julian method of computing time, the legal year commenced on Conception Day, the 25th of March. By the same calendar, the months were numbered as well as named. By the change from the Old Style to the New Style of reckoning, the date, April 14, 1658, O. S., would correspond in the new calendar, with April 24th, 1888, as to the day in the year. The O. S. was used in England until 1752, when the Gregorian year, or New Style, was adopted. See Webster's Dictionary—word "style."

Sarah had petitioned the General Court at Plymouth for letters of administration, but before they reached her, she, too, had died. The case was again taken under advisement, at a court held in Plymouth, March 5, 1684-5, and the following order was passed : " Whereas, administration was granted to Sarah Bartlett, relict of John Bartlett, late of Rehoboth, and an order to the Wors[h] Mr. Daniel Smith to take her oth to the inventory, but before there was oppertunity for soe doeing, said Sarah died, the Court therefore requests the Wors[h] Mr. Daniel Smith, together with the celect men of Rehoboth, to make enquiry for a fitte person to take out letters of administration on the estate, and that the younger children, by the said Mr. Smith, and the celect men of the towne, be disposed as may be most for theire good & least charge to the estate, and the estate be according to theire best judgment secured and improued for the benefitt of the orphanes, and that they giue accompt of theire actings and all matters relating to said children and estate to the next Court, and for theire confeirmation, and further settleing the children that ma chuse theire guardians, be sent to the General Court for approbation. And if a meete psn psent himself that will giue bond to adminnestration to the said pson, and giue oth to the inventory, and that hee make a return of his doeings to the next Court."

The estate was " inventoried and apprised by the Proprietors," February 26, 1684, and a copy sent to Plymouth, which is on record there. The following articles were mentioned in the inventory :

THE BARTLETT INVENTORY.

"Wearing apparel, Bedding, Wife's apparel and Linnen, Warming pan & pewter, Iron Potts & Possnett, Spinning Wheel Cards and Leather, Chests, Box & Linnen, Rundletts, Pails, and other Cooper's Wares, Trays, Dishes & Bromchors, Glass Bottles & Spoons, Pinchers, Knives, Awls, Hammers & Gambletts, Trowells, Tounges, Bellows & Chairs, Two Guns, Sword, Sickle, a Smoothing Iron, Yarn & Cloath, Earthen Pots, Bedding in the chamber, Saddle & Pillian, A Box Salt & a Chest with Carpenters' Tools, Weidges, Rings, Bridles, Halters, Axes & Hoes, Sulkies with their tackling and forks, Cart, Plow & Chains att, A Trapp on son by Information, A Raw Hidde, Swine, Two Oxen, Three Cows & two Heffers, a Mare & Colt, Ou Indian Corn, The House & fifty acres of land enclosed. The rest of the North Share undivided, Half a grist mill & five acres land adjoining on Providence side by Information." The whole of which was apprized at

£1301, 17s. 3p. " This is a just apprisement of the above said estate according to our understanding."

PETER HUNTE.

" John Bartlett & Mary Aldrich made oath to this Inventory the 19th
March, 1634-5, before Daniel Smith, Assistant."

JOHN PECK.
NICHOLAS PECK.

This was a large estate to have in those days, and this, too,
just after the close of that devastating war with King Phillip,
when all suffered such extreme losses.   At this time, nearly
every article of manufacture was imported from England, and
it had not been many years since their cows and horses were
received from the mother country.   And those " Sulkies and
their tackling ;" what a luxury !   For at that time almost the
only means of locomotion was by horseback.   The cows, so
useful for the dairy, were also brought into requisition at the
plow and cart,—very few settlers keeping oxen.   We can imag-
ine how some of the descendants would prize the sword mentioned in the inventory, were it in their possession to-day.
Bruised and bent and battered as it would be, it would be
very precious.   It may have done service for King Charles or
Cromwell.

John Bartlett's worldly possessions were much greater than
those of any others of the same name, and greater than most
of those of other names, who had then reached this country.
There is ample evidence that his children received educa-
tional treatment which few were able to enjoy, and it is regret-
able that they were orphaned among strangers, in a strange
land, at such a tender age.   It is not easy to comprehend the
hardships suffered, and difficulties overcome, by these courageous pioneers in this almost barren wilderness, where they
built their homes.   They were the sort of men who laid the
foundations of constitutional liberty, in great and free and
happy America.   All honor to them !

The estate of John Bartlett and wife was very likely held
in trust by the " Proprietors " until 1698.   At that time, the
children, except Noah and Daniel, not then of age, signed an
agreement for the distribution of the property, which had become impaired by providing for many young children during
the fourteen years which elapsed after the death of their par-

ents.   The following is a copy of the agreement recorded in the Bristol county probate office at Taunton, Mass. :

COPY OF AGREEMENT.

"Whereas, John Bartlett & Sarah Bartlett, sometime of Rehoboth, deceased in the year 1684, and leaving eight children behinde them & an estate undisposed on in lands & chattels, the children being under age & this estate not yett settled, We, the said children being severall of us, come to full age ; & being desirous to be invested of our generall rights in that estate of our said fathers, Have for and in Consideration of fifty acors of Land and afiftieth part of aright in Comonage, and fourteen pounds on shilling in Lawfull mony in hand already well and truly paid; to us by our elder brother John Bartlett, the rescipt whereof we doe own and acknowledgd, & therewith doe rest our selves flully sattisfied, Contented & paid, and doe by these presents for our selves, our heiors, executours & assignes flully & freely & absolutely exhonorate, aquitt & discharge our said Brother, John Bartlett, his heiors, executours & administratours & asignes & every of them off and frome every part & parcle of lands and monys ; before expressed these Children that have thus jointly & severally Agreed with ther Brother John Bartlett; are Samuell Bartlett, Moses Bartlett, Jacob Bartlett, Vallinctine Whiteman and Sarah Whiteman, his wife and Mary Bartlett ; Samuel Bartlett hath Agreed for the fifty acors of land and afiftieth part of aright in Comonage—; and Moses Bartlett, for four pounds, one shilling in mony, and Jacob Bartlett, for four pounds in mony and Vallintine Whiteman and Sarah, his wife, for three pounds in mony, and Mary Bartlett, for three pounds; flor and in Consideration of said lands & mony, we, the sd children before named, Haue Given, Granted, Bargained and sold, And doo by thes presents, Give, Grant, Bargaine, sell, alien enfeoffe, rattifie & Confirme unto our said Brother, John Bartlett, his heiors & executors, administratours and asignes for ever : all an singuler our rights, titles, interests, claimes or demands whatsoever that ever we had or have in or to the estate of our said father, John Bartlett, deceased : In wittness of the premises we haue jointly and seucrally sett to our hands and seales, this second day of January, 1698, or '99.

"And flurther the humble request of us who doe hereunto subscribe; is that the honored Mr. John Sailin, Esquire and Judg of probates of wils, would be pleased to accept of this our agreement and grant that a record may be made of the same.

	JOHN BARTLET,	[Seal.]
Signed, Seald & delivered	SAMUEL BARTLET,	[Seal.]
in presents of us :	JACOB BARTLET,	[Seal.]
	MOSES BARTLETT.	[Seal.]
JONATHAN SPRAGUE,	VALINTINE WHITMAN in behalf of	[Seal.]
ANTHONY SPRAGUE.	SARAH WHITMAN, his wife	
	MARY BARTLET.	[Seal.]"

FIRST RHODE ISLAND SETTLER.

Senechataconnet (Manville), where John Bartlett located when he removed from Mendon to Rehoboth, was only about four miles from William Blackstone's residence at Study Hill, so that John was near the home of the first known settler of Rhode Island. The river, on the bank of which William Blackstone established himself, bears his name.*

Anything concerning the town of Cumberland, or Rehoboth, would be incomplete without mention of this singular man, who had also been the first settler of Shawmut (Boston), and who shunned the intolerance and bigotry of the puritanical polity, as something more to be dreaded than Indian treachery, or the hardships of the wilderness. His biography is in no way connected, so far as known, with that of the personages of the Bartlett genealogy. But there is a propriety in introducing a few points of interest regarding the man whose character must have markedly impressed itself upon his neighbors. Some account of his residence will be of interest.†

During the summer of 1877, the writer chanced to be in the vicinity of this historic place and spent some time in looking over the ground. The hill where William Blackstone had fitted up a place for study, and by him denominated " Study Hill," is very near the depot of the Providence and Worcester railroad, at Lonsdale, a few steps south. Very little of the original hill remains, the railroad being located nearly through its center. It must have been a beautiful site. The river here makes a graceful bend, flowing near the base of the hill, with picturesque effect. A few rods east of the hill is the place where his house is supposed to have stood, although the spot is not ascertained with precision. A little brook of clear, sparkling water, is very near, and a fine, level piece of land in proximity could have served him as a lawn, over which he passed in going to, and coming from, his study on the hill. Several apple-trees now stand near the site of the house and they are, no doubt, the offspring of those he planted.

---

* There were, at different times, other names given to it, but finally it was permanently named the Blackstone. Some of the earlier names were "Pawtucket," "Great River," " Kattatuck," "Nipmuck," " Seacouk," "Senechataconnet," and there were others.
† This place where Mr. Blackstone lived was called by the Indians, " Wawepoonseag."

His grave is pointed out in a spot very near, and between the house and the hill, but it is not certain that his body was buried there. The supposed grave is marked by two stones, their oval tops showing above the ground, and at the usual distance between head-stones and foot-stones. It is apparent that these stones were placed there for a purpose, because there are no other stones of any kind near the place. The following is copied from the Rehoboth records :

" Sarah Blaxton, wife of William, buried about the middle of June, 1673. William Blaxton, buried 28th May, 1675."

A few days after his death the Indian war commenced and his dwelling house was burned. The records at Plymouth contain an inventory of his estate, including 184 books, which constituted his library. Among them may have been manuscripts, which, if preserved, would give information concerning his life and observations, of which little is known. After his removal to Cumberland—then Rehoboth—it appears, by the Boston town records, that : "Mr. William Blackstone was married to Sarah Stevenson, widow, the 4th of July, 1659, by John Endicott, Governor." She was the widow of John Stevenson, by whom she had several children. One son, John Stevenson, Jr., lived with his mother in Cumberland after her marriage with Blackstone, and the Court at Plymouth, in consideration of " his services to his parents," granted him a part of Mr. Blackstone's land " during the remainder of his life."

It is not known whether this marriage with Mrs. Stevenson was his first, or not. By her, he had one son—John—who resided on his estate until 1692, when he sold his land to Daniel Whipple and removed to Providence, where, it is said, he followed the occupation of a shoemaker. The town records of Providence show that he had born, while living there, a son named John Blackstone, Jr., who was adopted by Richard Wicks. There is a tradition that a son of John, and grandson of William Blackstone, while serving in the French war, as Lieutenant, was killed, at the taking of Louisburg If correct, the Lieutenant may have been this adopted child. It has been stated, by some writers, that the Connecticut Blackstones are descended from William, but the records do not show such relationship. After the settlement of Providence by Roger Williams, William Blackstone often went there to preach, and it is related that, in old age, he made the journey on the back of a tame, white bull. " This novel *bulgine* " is said to have created much amusement for the younger part of the population, to whom on such occasions he often distributed apples (quite rare in those days) which he brought from his farm—the produce of the trees he had planted. His removal from Boston was the occasion of the remarks, often quoted, which reveal his desire for independence. " I came from England," he said, "because I did not like the Lords' Bishops, but I cannot join with you because I would not be under the Lord's brethren."

The difficulty which he found in living with the Lords' Bishops of England, and which he gave as the reason for coming to this country, and again, the difficulty he mentioned of living at peace with the Lord's brethren at Boston, appears to have dominated at Study Hill, and the court records tell of many misunderstandings with neighbors, who, he persistently imagined, were trying to encroach upon him and deprive him of his rights. The testimony points to the fact that William Blackstone, with all his really commendable traits of character, which, very likely, were in advance of the age in which he lived, had a very quarrelsome and turbulent temper. He certainly manifested bad judgment in so conspicuously differing with every one with whom he came in contact. The Lords' Bishops and Lord's brethren, who appear to have been so obnoxious to him, not only controlled the church, but also state affairs, and there was such a blending of religious and civic interests that an offence against either called for the exercise of the executive department of law.

We hear much of the intolerance and bigotry of those rulers who banished Roger Williams, caused Quakers and witches to be hung, and sensitive women to be whipped for their religious opinions, but when we consider the fanatical zeal with which the ignorant and superstitious intruded their diversified ideas of religious duty upon society, it is apparent that a rigid, legal restraint was necessary for the preservation of the morals of the community. Only one illustration will

show the necessity of prompt and severe action by the
authorities. At Salem, a *sensitive* Quaker woman conceived it
to be a religious duty to dispense with the use of clothing, and
she exhibited herself in nudity upon the streets. The teachings
of the Pilgrims at Plymouth had borne fruit. The religious
liberty of which they were the exponents, was construed with
such liberality that transgressors of the law, under the guise
of religion, sought to shield themselves by eccentric behavior,
and doctrine, from the penalty of their crimes. Had Roger
Williams, in the unsettled state of society, been actuated with
a desire to promote the peace, and good order, of the colony,
he could have done much good in directing and influencing
the public mind, but, with a selfish disregard of the welfare of
the community, he labored to intensify the feeling of religious
speculation and controversy. It has been the custom to extol
and eulogize the man, and write contemptuous things touching the commonwealth which chose to protect itself by
banishing its mischief makers, but it is reasonable to believe
that had he not happened to be the nucleus of a subsequent
colonization, he would never have been heard of, except in connection with other offenders, who suffered punishment for their
incontumacy and crimes, committed, as his was, in violation
of true religious principles and the interests of society, and in
defiance of the customs, usages, and laws, of the government
to which he had sworn allegiance. While this introductory
matter, and its interpolations, is somewhat discursive, an excuse
for digression from the main feature of the work is found in the
circumstance that most of the men, especially those of promi-
nence herein mentioned, had no doubt been met on different
occasions by John Bartlett, and he was certainly familiar with
the controversies, and suffered by the wars and adversities
which afflicted the early inhabitants. Therefore, anything
which agitated and alarmed the public mind, during his life,
was to him a personal matter, and, as such, may assist the im-
agination in its conception of his character and surroundings.
There being so little known concerning him, it has been
taken for granted that these things, although indirect, will, in
this connection, be interesting to his descendants. The tradition that he was in London during the great fire of Septem-

ber, 1666, (O. S.) would appear not improbable, as it was five
months after that date when he was in Weymouth.   The
destruction of his home by the fire may have been the
immediate cause of his emigration to this country, but this,
together with many other things concerning him, and his
wife, Sarah, and their antecedents, which it would be a grati-
fication to know, must for the present be left to conjecture;
but it is hoped that a future scion of the stock will be fortunate in learning all that is now in obscurity regarding the
personal history and career of this pioneer.

EXPLANATION.

The simplest possible plan has been adopted to facilitate
the tracing of lines of descent.   The number placed at the
left, and preceding the name of a child, signifies that the person
will appear on a subsequent page as a parent, designated by
the same number.

The notes and record transcripts for this book were com-
piled in 1879, but, in a few instances, there are records of a
later date.

JOHN BARTLETT.

John Bartlett and his wife Sarah were at Weymouth, Mass., before 1666. In 1671 he had removed to Mendon, Mass., and was there in 1679 and 1682. June 6, 1682, he bought land and removed to the place called Senechetaconnet, which, at that time, was in the town of Rehoboth and under the jurisdiction of the Plymouth Colony, but now known as Manville, in the town of Cumberland and State of Rhode Island,— where he died August 17, 1684. Sarah, his wife, died the following January, 1684–5.

CHILDREN OF JOHN BARTLETT.

1. JOHN, b. Feb. 11, 1666, in Weymouth.
2. SAMUEL, b. ——; m. Sarah Inman, Dec., 19, 1695.
3. JACOB, b. ——; m. Sarah ——.
4. MOSES, b. ——; m. Deborah (widow of Abraham) Harding.

   SARAH, b. ——; m. Captain Valentine Whitman, Jr., Dec. 19, 1694, in Providence, R. I. He was born Aug. 28, 1665, a son of Valentine and Mary Whitman.* He was a Captain in the Militia and held many positions of trust in civil life. He and his wife, Sarah Bartlett, had the following children born in Providence, viz.: *Sarah*, b. June 26, 1696, d. 1698; *John*, b. Feb. 20, 1698; *Henry*, b. Jan. 16, 1700; *Abiah*, b. Jan. 4, 1707–8; *Robert*, b. May 2, 1712; *Benjamin*, b. July 22, 1715; *Noah*, b. Dec. 31, 1717; and a *daughter*.

   MARY, b. Jan. 1, 1679. [*Mendon records.*]

   NOAH, b. Jan. 29, 1680. [*Mendon records.*]

5. DANIEL, b. Jan. 24, 1684. [*Rehoboth records.*]

*Valentine Whitman, Sr., was in Providence before 1650, was chosen surveyor, 1671; he was commissioner to treat with the Indians, 1657; constable, 1659; in 1661, was chosen to divide the land. He was very prominent in the affairs of the town and appeared to be the Miles Standish of the colony, especially as related to the Indians, with whom he acted as interpreter, and was often called upon to settle differences with them. He was elected to the Legislature in 1673 and 1685. He died, January 20, 1701. His wife, Mary, died May 31, 1718. He and his wife Mary had Mary, b. 1652, m. John Inman; Elizabeth, b. 1655, Susanna, b. 1656, m. 1683, James Bakon; Valentine, Jr., b. 1668, m. Sarah Bartlett.

(1.) JOHN BARTLETT[2] (*John*[1])

He was b. Feb. 11, 1666, in Weymouth, Mass., and was the eldest son ; m. Alice——.   He d. Nov. 8, 1732.   She d. the same year.   In 1708–9, he purchased of William Sabin*, one of the original proprietors of the Rehoboth, North Purchase, 200 acres of land.   He was allotted land also, 1714, and 1727, by the "Proprietors."†   These additions to the estate which he had purchased from his brothers and sisters, in the settlement of his father's estate, 1698, made him an extensive land-owner, even for those times; for he had, altogether, nearly a thousand acres, nearly all of which abutted the Blackstone river, on the west, and lay between what is now Manville and Cumberland Hill, R. I.   He was surveyor of highways, constable, member of the town council, etc.‡

CHILDREN.

ALICE, b. Oct. 16, 1688; m. John Cass.

SARAH, b. Oct. 25, 1690: m. John Balcom, whom she outlived.   She died Nov. 19, 1756.   In her will she mentions "my cousin Caleb, son of my brother, John ; Alice, wife of John Cass ; my brother, Jeremiah Bartlett ; Ebenezer Darling, son of my sister, Martha ; my sister, Mrs. Hannah Staples ; cousin Martha, daughter of my brother, Ezra; and Richard, son of my brother, Ezra: and my cousin Susannah Jillson."   She also gave a sum of money to Elder Nathaniel Cook, toward repairing the Baptist Meeting House, in Smithfield, which stood by Benjamin Cook's.§

    SUSANNAH, b. Aug. 24, 1692.

6.   JOHN,‖ b. June 8, 1694.

7.   JOB, b. July 6, 1697.

    MARTHA, b. March 10, 1699; m. first, Robert Staples, June 23, 1730 ; m. second, Ebenezer Darling, and had by him a son, Ebenezer, and perhaps other children.

8.   JEREMIAH, b. May 9, 1701.

9.   EZRA, b. April 4, 1703.

    HANNAH, b. June 7, 1706 ; m. Joseph Staples.

*The same from whom John Bartlett, Sr., purchased his first land at Shummasetaconet, now Manville, R. I., June 6, 1682.

†Proprietors' rec., Attleboro.

‡Attleboro town rec.

§Smithfield rec.

‖ The first four children are recorded in the Rehoboth rec., the others in Attleborough.

(2.) SAMUEL BARTLETT[2] (*John*[1]).

Born ——— ; m. Mary, dau. of John and Mary* (Whitman) Inman, Dec. 19, 1695. Made his will, Feb. 24, 1742-3 ; d. about 1743. He was surveyor of highways, 1702; constable, 1706 ; his tax in 1707 was the largest of any one's in town, with one exception. [*Attleboro records*.] He bought of Samuel Shrouds, or Shoreds, July 1, 1697, a parcel of land on Peetar's River, in Dedham, lying between Mendon and Attleboro. In 1714, his brother John gave him land adjoining his own at Shunnasetaconnet, now Manville, R. I., and he also bought several tracts of fifty and twenty-five acres each, abutting that given him, so that he had quite a snug farm at that place. In addition to other public office held by him at different times, he was a justice of the peace.

CHILDREN.

10. SAMUEL, b. Oct. 9, 1696; m. Mary Aldrich, Dec. 8, 1717.
     JERUSHA, b. May 3, 1698.
11. NOAH, b. April 22, 1700; m. Susana Lovett, Sept. 19, 1722.
     MARY, b. Jan. 5, 1708-9; m. —— Smith; had (probably) Mary and Noah; d. before 1742.

(3.) JACOB BARTLETT[2] (*John*[1]).

Born ——— : m. Sarah ———. He bought, Oct. 29, 1696, a " nine cows' commonage," from James Albee, of Mendon, described in the deed as being between Mendon and Wrentham, adjoining the Plymouth line,† and was an undivided right in the common lands. Jacob had been living in Providence prior to this time, and it is probable that he very soon after the purchase of this land, settled on it. The Bellingham records‡

*Mary, wife of John Inman, was sister of Captain Valentine Whitman Jr., who married Sarah Bartlett. John Inman and his wife, Mary (Whitman) Inman, had *Mary*, who married the above Samuel Bartlett; *John, Valentine, Deborah, Tabitha*, and *Joanna*, who never married, and died at the house of Valentine Whitman. There was also one daughter, who married —— Matthewson.

†It will be remembered that, Cumberland, at that time, was partly settled and belonged to Plymouth.

‡Bellingham was incorporated Nov. 27, 1719, from parts of Dedham, Wrentham, and Meadon.

inform us that, Oct. 27, 1713, the first land laid out in that part of Dedham lying west of Wrentham, and east of Mendon— it being land granted by the General Court, 1662, to Mendon— was " 36 acres to Jacob Bartlett, who had settled on ye land before laid out." July 26, 1713, he had laid out from Josiah Thayer, 36 acres, and Nov. 15, 1723, more land abutting his own was laid out to him near Iron Rock Brook, and seven acres were granted him in another place, one acre and fifty-six rods being allowed for bad land ; also, same date, 1 acre and 100 rods were laid out to him, in lieu of land taken from his homestead, by Banfield Capron, in the fourth division. His purchases of land were numerous, and not confined to any particular locality. The last conveyances recorded by him, and the last record of any kind concerning him, are two deeds to his sons, Jacob, Jr., and Joseph, in 1737-8, " in considera-tion of love which he bore his son, Joseph," he deeded him " three tracts, or parcels, of land," in Bellingham.* " One piece, the homestead, where I now dwell, thirty acres, it being all the land I have lying together at that place, together with the dwelling house and buildings thereon." The second piece consisted of ten acres, lying southerly of the homestead, and adjoining land of his son, Jacob,—all the land he had at that place. The third piece was one-half of thirty acres, bounded on the east, by Richard Aldrich and Nathaniel Jillson; south-east and south, by Uriah Jillson, and northeast, by Samuel Staples. Witnessed by Abner Bartlett, and acknowledged by Jacob, Sr., at Worcester, Mass., March 7, 1737-38, and recorded in Cumberland, April 20, 1747. In consideration of 50 lbs. current money, he sold his son, Jacob, Jr., of Providence, a part of his homestead, Nov. 24, 1737. Acknowledged by Jacob, Sr., personally, at Worcester, Mass., March 7, 1737-8. Witnessed by Joseph Bartlett, and recorded in Cumberland, April 11, 1747.

*The land was in the disputed territory, and was claimed at that time by both the Massa-chusetts and Plymouth governments, and the residents did not know whether they were in Bellingham or Attleboro, the present town of Cumberland at that time belonging to Attleboro, and called " Attleboro Gore." The boundaries were established, and Jan. 27, 1746-7, the town was incorporated, being named after Cumberland, England. It was annexed to Provi-dence County, Feb. 17, 1746-7.

This land was described as being near the Iron Rock Meadow, and bounded by land of Nathaniel Jillson, and —— Ingalls, and on the south by Francis Inman. These were, probably, his last conveyances, and perhaps he lived afterward with his son, Joseph, to whom he gave his house, etc., for he was at this time advanced in years. It is not known at what time he died. He was a Quaker, and so were his sons, and this circumstance explains why there were no gravestones found with inscriptions, in the old Bartlett burying ground. The society of Friends, or Quakers, did not allow anything of that kind, it being a principle with them not to distinguish one person more than another. Some modification has taken place in the rules then prevailing, for, at the present time, they permit the friends of a deceased person to erect very plain stones, with brief inscriptions.

A few persons of other than the Bartlett name were buried in the Bartlett burying ground. It is situated on the east side of the lane leading from the old Livin Bartlett place, now (1879) owned by Leprelet Miller, on the Woonsocket road, to the homestead house, where Joseph, son of Jacob, lived and died, and which Jacob, probably, built when he settled there in 1696. The house is still standing, in a good state of preservation, and, with its huge timbers and substantial workmanship, will defy the ravages of time for many years. The house and farm are now (1879) owned by George Waterman, who kindly allowed the writer while on a visit to the place, to take from one of the doors the old hinges and wooden latch which I have attached to a board, ornamented and painted for the purpose, and deposited them in the headquarters of the Society of Antiquity, Worcester, Mass. The hinges are very old style, and show the wear of nearly two centuries of use. They were, perhaps, made at Jacob's establishment, as he was a manufacturer of hardware and edge-tools, as well as a farmer. The burying ground is fast disappearing, and in a few years the encroachments which are being made, year after year, will have obliterated every object which marks the last resting place of these plain, virtuous, Christian saints. There can still be seen about two dozen rough grave-stones,—Quaker-fashion,—although nearly obscured by shrubs and grass. It

is probable that Jacob was buried in this ground, as well as
many of his descendants.

CHILDREN

(Of Jacob[1] and Sarah Bartlett).

> DAMIRIAH,[|] b. ——; m. Obadiah Ballou, Jan. 5, 1717-18. She
> died between 1738 and 1740. [*Providence records.*]
>
> MOSES, b. ——. He was admitted freeman of Gloucester, 1736.
> He had land on the branch of the Pawtucket River, in Smith-
> field, side of his brother, Abner. Sold it to his Uncle Moses,
> of Providence, Jan. 30, 1735-6. Jacob, Jr., owned land at the
> same place.
>
> 12. ABNER, b. ——; m. Abigail Arnold, April 30, 1734.[‡]
> 13. JACOB, JR., b. ——; m. first, Sarah ——; second, Lydia Muzzy,
>   Oct. 20, 1742; daughter of James Muzzy, of Mendon, Mass.
> 14. JOSEPH, b. ——; m. Abigail Aldrich, Nov. 7, 1744.

(4.) MOSES BARTLETT[2] (*John[1]*).

Was born ——; married Deborah, widow of Abraham Harding. He lived in Providence, R. I. At a meeting of the town
council of Providence, held March 3, 1695-6, letters of administration were granted to Deborah Harding, widow of Abraham, deceased, to administer to his estate, " and whereas she
had lately changed her name and condition by marriage with
Moses Bartlett," it was asked that they might jointly administer the said estate, and it was granted " that said Moses and
Deborah should jointly administer untill the day of their next
meeting, and then to appear before said counsel and render
their accounts and give bonds for further administration."
Moses made oath to an inventory, 1694. He was constable,
1696. He had laid out, in 1706, by the " Proprietors," on the
original right of Benjamin Smith, 110 acres on the west side
of the seven mile line at Nipgachuck. In 1708, he had 36

---

[1] It is singular that none of Jacob's children have their births recorded in the town records.
And it does not appear that the dates of their births are known. Whether this absence of record
was owing to the imperfect manner in which the records of the town were kept, or was the result
of the Quaker capriciousness in such matters, which prevailed at that early period, can only be
conjectural. His being in the disputed territory, not knowing in which town he belonged, undoubtedly affected the registration of births, as well as the recording of deeds, and other legal
documents.

[|] Spelled in one place, " Dea m-a-r-i-s."

[‡] Abner Bartlett, being a Quaker, was exempt from taxation, August 22, 1731. A Jacob
Bartlett was published to Charity Inman, Aug. 29, 1741. Jacob Bartlett, being an Anabaptist,
was exempt from taxes for ministerial purposes, July 18, 1734. *Bellingham records.*]

acres more laid out to him, adjoining the 110 acres before laid
out. September 27, 1721, there were two acres on the east
side of the seven-mile line, at Huckleberry Hill, "adjoining a
great cleft of rocks," laid out to him. [*Proprietors' records*,
Providence.] He had, previously, March 14, 1719–20, bought
of Andrew Harris, land at "Huckleberry Hill," 20 acres on
the "northward and eastward," part of the hill near the "great
common," and on the north side of the road, and "nine and one-
half acres" on the south side of the road. [*Providence Reg. of
deeds*, Book 4, page 143.] His land conveyances are very
numerous. He was often buying and selling. His residence
is described as being one and a half miles from the center of
the town, the center being then, as now, Weybossett bridge.
It was on the east side of the "seven-mile line,"* bordering on
the "stated common and at the junction of the Plainfield and
Killingly roads"—between those roads. He was a very face-
tious and intelligent man, of very positive opinions, and fear-
lessly advocated what he believed to be right.

He was, undoubtedly, a strong temperance man, for he sold
land in 1725, and stipulated in his deed that "there shall be
no house of entertainment, nor any strong drinks sold upon the
premises forever." This being at a time when prohibition had
not been heard of, and when nearly all men used alcohol in
some form, indicates that he was in advance of his neighbors,
and was an original and independent thinker, who acted according to his convictions. He was a Quaker for many years, but
the tight-jacket creed of that sect, at the time, did not harmon-
ize with his impulsive and aggressive nature, and in 1741, he
took a "new departure," on account of entertaining religious
opinions which the stern and rigid old Quakers looked upon
with consternation and holy horror. He issued a challenge,
Nov. 9, 1741, to the Baptists and Quakers, to meet him and
argue their doctrines, or else lie under the charge of "preach-
ing the doctrines of the devil."

This challenge appeared in the *Boston Gazette* of that
date.†

---

* This seven-mile line was established in 1660. It was the western boundary of the early
division of the Providence town lands; afterwards they divided on the west side. The line ran
on what is now the eastern boundary of Scituate, Gloucester, and Burrillville.

† Arnold's History of Rhode Island, Vol. II, pp. 137–8.

It appears from the records of the Smithfield Monthly Meeting of Quakers, to which he belonged, that expostulation did him no good, and he did not " succeede " in converting them to his belief, nor they in convincing him that they were just right. So he was finally excommunicated from that society, 30th 2nd mo., 1741. He appears to have sold all his land before 1750, and gone to live with his brother, Daniel, in Gloucester.* He had attained an age of nearly four score years, and had doubtless settled up his business, well knowing that his stewardship on earth was nearly at an end.

He died in Gloucester, Jan. 25, 1753. His will was made, 25 Dec. 1752. In his bequests, he gives his cousin [nephew], Jacob Bartlett, £1279, his cloak, china-ware, etc. " To brother Daniel Bartlett, all my wearing apparel, except my cloak." " To my cousin [nephew], Daniel Aldrich, grandson to my brother, Daniel Bartlett, all my silver money and bound books." " To my brother Daniel Bartlett's two daughters, Joanna Aldrich, and Sarah Inman, all my beds and bedding." To Moses Bartlett, son of his nephew, Job Bartlett, he gave all his plate marked with the two letters of his name—M. B. He had, before this—Oct. 9, 1751—made a deed, which was recorded in Cumberland, giving Job's son, Moses, the plate marked with his initials, as mentioned in the will—and " one great silver pot," and " one pint silver cup, with two handles, two tea spoons, and three silver spoons, one Job has in his possession already ; one spoon, the bowl of gold." All these were to be taken into custody, after his death, " by the owner of said child," and if the said child did not live to be of age, these things were " to be given to the next of Job's posterity," who should " bear the name of Moses " He, probably, had no children living at the time of his death, and it is not known that he ever had any, as none are mentioned in his will, and it is conjectured that his wife died several years before ; it may be, about the time of his removal to Gloucester.

His wife had a son, John Harding, by her first marriage with Abraham Harding.

*He also lived awhile in Cumberland.

(5.) DANIEL BARTLETT² (*John¹*).

Born Jan. 24, 1684 * [*Rehoboth records.*] He lived in Mendon, Mass., and afterward, in Gloucester, R. I. He was admitted freeman of Gloucester, 1738. He married, first, Mary —— ; second, Abigail Tucker, Sept. 25, 1749.† He sold his right in the undivided lands of Attleboro, to his brother, John, Feb. 14, 1722 ; he was then living in Wrentham, Mass. He made his will, Feb. 8, 1759, and died, June, 29, 1762, in Gloucester. His will mentions his daughter, Joanna, wife of Jacob Aldrich, and his daugher, Mary, wife of Job Bartlett ; also, Sarah Inman, wife of Abraham Inman. These are, probably, all the children he had. His will was witnessed by Abner Bartlett.

CHILDREN.

JOHANNAH, b. March 18, 1713, by wife, Mary. [*Mendon records.*]
Johannah m. July 3, 1731, Jacob Aldrich, of Uxbridge, Mass. They had one son —Daniel—and, perhaps, others.
MARY, b. March 8, 1715, by wife, Mary. [*Mendon records.*]
Mary married her cousin, Job Bartlett, May 27, 1733.
SARAH, b. ——; m. Abraham Inman, Aug. 13, 1736.

(6.) JOHN BARTLETT³ (*John²*; *John¹*).

Born June 8, 1694 ; m. Sarah Aldrich, Oct. 15, 1738, and died about 1754. His wife survived him some years.

CHILDREN.

SARAH, b. March 15, 1738 ; m. William Emerson.
CALEB, b. July 24, 1741. He was a farmer, and lived some time in Providence, R. I. He owned land in Cumberland, both sides of the Mendon road, at a point where the Wrentham road leads out of it. [*Cumberland records.*]
ANNA, b. Aug. 28, 1746; d. July 27, 1749.
There may have been other children.

[In the Suffolk register of Probate, is this: "John Bartlett, deceased, wife, Sarah, letters of administration granted to his son, *Peter*. He died before 1754. He had a son, *John*, and daughters, *Mary, Sarah, Hannah, Ann, Abigail, Esther*, and *Eliz.*" This may be the family above. T. E. B.]

* He was about six months old when his parents died.

† A Daniel Bartlett married Patience, daughter of Thomas and Patience (Cook) Arnold [*Richardson's History of Woonsocket.*]

(7.) JOB BARTLETT[3] (*John[2]*; *John[1]*).

Born July 6, 1697; m. his cousin, Mary, daughter of Daniel
Bartlett, of Smithfield, May 27, 1733. His homestead was
situated on the great river—Blackstone—near Sennacheta-
connet. He was a lawyer of great ability, and a leading
spirit in all town affairs. He was made a constable, 1723, and
selectman, 1726. [*Attleboro records.*] Was admitted a freeman of Gloucester, April 3, 1745. At the incorporation of
the town of Cumberland, Jan. 27, 1746-7, he was chosen the
first Town Clerk, and the first records are in his hand-writing.
He was chosen Justice of the Peace at the same time, and
held the office until his death. Many are the marriages at
which he officiated as the Justice, young people from far and
near coming to him to tie the nuptial knot. It is assumed
that he did this service very acceptably, or his assistance
would not have been in such great request. For many years,
at every meeting of the town or council, his name was con-
spicuous, and his services as "Moderator" were considered
indispensable, as no one else was ever chosen to that place
when he was present. He was elected Representative, 1747,
being the first Representative of the town in the General
Assembly—or Legislature—of Rhode Island, and served,
annually, until 1756, and was again elected to the same position in 1757, 1759, and 1763. At the first meeting of the
town, after its incorporation, the prominent offices were filled
by persons named Bartlett, and the fact that the Bartletts were
so active in the administration of town affairs, and that the
public business appeared to have been done so systematically,
and such accurate records of all transactions were kept, will
cause a feeling of pride in their descendants. In the many
towns where the writer of this has had occasion to examine
the records of their early proceedings, there are no records so
well kept as those of Cumberland : and this good beginning
has been an example for the generations which have followed.
Even to the present day, under the efficient care of Mr. Horace
Follet, Town Clerk, the books and records of the town are
models of neatness and accuracy. The town was indebted to
Job Bartlett for the advanced position which it took among

the other towns of the State, immediately after its incorporation. He made his will, Aug. 15, 1765, and died the next
year. His widow survived him for some years. His son, John,
was administrator of the estate.

CHILDREN.

15. JOHN, b. May 14, 1734; m. Deborah Phillips. He was a surgeon
general in the Revolution.
JOB, b. Feb., 29, 1735-6; d. young.
DANIEL, b. Feb. 2, 1737-8.
HANNAH, b. Nov. 8, 1739-40; d. young.
JEMIMA, b. July 2, 1742; m. Samuel Chamberlin.
16. JOB, b. June 9, 1744; m. Molly Ramsdell.
MARTHA, b. April 11, 1746; m. Uriah Carpenter, of Gloucester.
HANNAH, b. Feb. 4, 1747; never married.
MOSES, b. March 24, 1749-50.
PHEBE, b. April 22, 1753; never married.

(8.) JEREMIAH BARTLETT[3] (John[2]; John[1]).

Born May 9, 1701; m., May 15, 1730, Margret Tower. He
was chosen assessor at the first town meeting of Cumberland,
Feb. 10, 1746, and, at different times afterward, held other
important offices. His land adjoined his brother John's, at
Senechataconnett (Manville). He died June 18, 1750, intes-
tate. His wife, Margret, was administrator.*

CHILDREN.

ALLIS, b. April 23, 1731; m. John Cass.
SARAH, b. Dec. 15, 1733.
MARGRET, b. July 31, 1735.
17. JEREMIAH, b. Aug. 16, 1741.
S......., b. Oct. 26, 1743.
A......., b. June 30, 1745.†

(9.) EZRA BARTLETT[3] (John[2]; John[1]).

Born April 4, 1703; m. Jane, daughter of Richard Lewis,
of Providence, Sept. 9, 1728. Ezra and his wife were
"Friends,"—Quakers—and were married while in that asso-

---

*He was, probably, buried in the old burying ground, about half way between Manville
and Cumberland Hill. There is a stone there, with the inscription just discernible, and on it:
" J. B., 1750." He was a Quaker.

†One of the daughters married Stephen Staples.

ciation. He was made a freeman of Providence, R. I., May 6, 1729. He bought, of William Hawkins, June 7, 1728, twenty acres of land on the Providence side, on the west of the seven-mile line, and had, also, land laid out to him by the Proprietors of Providence, the same year, near "Levill Plain ;" and some years afterward, had land laid out to him on the northeast side of Mantore's Lake, which may have been in what was afterward Gloucester,* for this was the town in which he afterward lived and died. He carried on the business of blacksmithing, as well as farming. He was often elected to office, being, at different times, town sergeant, surveyor, councilman, etc. He died, August 30, 1778. His will mentions one daughter, who married a —— Harendeen, and another also married a —— Coomans.

CHILDREN.

EZRA, b. August 30, 1729; m. Amey Thornton, Nov. 25, 1750, and d. May 17, 1755. His wife, Amey, was administrator.

ALICE, b. Oct. 14, 1733.

ANNIE, b. Aug. 6, 1736; m. Zebediah Mitchell, Dec. 29, 1754.

18. RICHARD, b. Feb. 28, 1738; m. Kezia ——.

DANIEL, b. Dec. 2, 1741. A grandson, Daniel, was living in Eastford, Conn., in 1877.

MARTHA, b. ——.

(10.) SAMUEL BARTLETT[3] (Samuel[2]; John[1]).

He was born October 9, 1696; m. Mary Aldrich, Dec. 8, 1717. At the first town meeting of Cumberland, he was chosen town treasurer, and held the office until his death, about 1755. He was also a constable and justice of the peace. [Attleboro records.] He was elected to the General Assembly — Legislature—of Rhode Island several terms, serving in that body, with Job Bartlett, in looking after the town's interests. He was an extensive farmer, and also did a large blacksmithing business.† His homestead was near the

*Gloucester was taken from Providence and incorporated Feb. 20, 1730-31.

†Blacksmithing, in those days, was an art requiring much more mechanical skill, and technical knowledge, than is needed at this time, when almost everything made of iron and used in constructive work, is produced by the aid of machinery. A blacksmith was obliged to make from crude materials—even from the ore itself—almost everything of iron needed in every department of industry and household convenience. All was wrought out, each thing by itself, involving an extensive acquaintance with form, strength of material, and the like. The articles made by the Bartletts who were engaged in manufacturing, were, axes, scythes, hoes, forks, shovels, etc., and, in fact, almost everything that was made of iron; the market for which was found in New York, Boston, Providence, Worcester, and other places.

other Bartletts at Senechetaconnet. At his father's death, he was appointed administrator.

CHILDREN.

> CHARLES, b. Sept. 21, 1727. Was a freeman of Cumberland, 1749. He was a soldier at Fort William Henry, Lake George, and died there, in January, 1756.
>
> MARY, b. ——; m., Feb. 2, 1764, John Fisk, of Cumberland.

(11.) NOAH BARTLETT[3] (*Samuel*[2]; *John*[1]).

Born April 22, 1700; m. Susannah Lovett, Sept. 19, 1722. He bought, of John Inman, Sept. 9, 1721, eighty acres of land on the Providence side, and "on the east side of the seven-mile line, and north of the river called Comstock branch, a little down the stream from where the Oxford road crosses the stream, and lying on the side of the stream." This land he sold to Joseph Smith, Feb. 26, 1722-3. [*Smithfield records.*] He also had land at Shunnasettaconnett. He made his will Sept. 25, 1752. His wife was appointed administrator. She became delirious in 1762, and was placed under the guardian-ship of her son, Israel, and James Cargill. Noah held differ-ent town offices.

CHILDREN.

> 19. NOAH, b. March 9, 1723; m. Elizabeth Phillips.
>
> SUSANNAH, b. April 21, 1725; m. —— Jillson.
>
> RUTH, b. Jan. 25, 1729; d. Sept. —, 1771.
>
> CHRISTOPHER,* b. Dec. —, 1732. He went to Mt. Desert, Me., 1755. He was a soldier in the French war, and served as lieu-tenant in the war of the Revolution.
>
> SAMUEL, b. Jan. 27, 1735.
>
> 20. ISRAEL, b. April 5, 1737; m. Caroline Balcom. Removed to Mt. Desert, Me., 1755. He was a soldier in the French and Revo-lutionary wars.
>
> 21. JEHO, b. June 16, 1739; m. Sarah Hadway. He settled in Sutton, and was sometimes called "John."

Christopher had Dea. d., et. 17, Christopher d., et. 16, Samuel d., et. 45, Elias d., et. 62, Isaac, Sallie d., et. 29, Hannah d., et. 2, Mary d., et. 43, Lucy d., et. 91. [From David J. Bartlett, of Pretty Marsh, Mt. Desert, Me.]

(12.) ABNER BARTLETT[3] (*Jacob*[2]; *John*[1]).

Married Abigail, daughter of John Arnold, April 30, 1734. She was, probably, of Uxbridge, where they inherited land from the woman's father, which they sold to John Harris, Oct 17, 1760. [*Worcester County Reg. of deeds.*] Abigail was b. 1711 ; d. 1815, at the age of 104 years.* Abner Bartlett located first in Bellingham, Mass., his place adjoining that of his father, and there was a highway laid out on this land, March 22, 1737. [*Bellingham records.*] He soon removed to Gloucester, and had land bought of Joseph Buffum, at the Branch, and which abutted Edward Inman's mill at that place. He was admitted a freeman of Gloucester, May 4, 1742. Was selectman from 1743 to 1750, and member of the town council; also surveyor of highways. He was a farmer, and carried on blacksmithing, and belonged to the Society of Friends—Quakers. He made his will, 23d Nov., 1784, and died the 13th of the following month, Dec. 13, 1784, leaving his estate to his wife, Abigail, and their three sons.

CHILDREN.

22. RUFUS, b. Nov. 16, 1739 ; m. Margaret Smith.
23. ELISHA, b. Sept. 7, 1742 ; m. Ruth Arnold.
24. CALEB, b. Jan. 19, 1745 ; m. Susannah Wilson.
     ANNIE, b. —— ; no issue.

(13.) JACOB BARTLETT, JR.,[3] (*Jacob*[2]; *John*[1]).

Married first, Sarah —— ; second, Lydia, dau. of James Muzzy, of Mendon, Oct. 20, 1742. His cousin [uncle] Moses, of Providence, gave him, April 24, 1734, his homestead land, "where I now dwell, with all the housings thereon, and one acre nearer the town, where the highways part," and another piece on the north side of "Huckleberry Hill." He did not stay long with his uncle. Sept. 22, 1737, he sold the property back to him, and returned to Cumberland and Bellingham, and bought, Nov. 24, 1737, for £50, a part of his father's homestead, and carried on the business of making scythes, and

---

* John Arnold, father of Abner's wife, was son of Richard Arnold, who d. 1710, and grandson of Thomas Arnold, who d. Sept. 1674. [*Bassell Memorial.*]

other things connected with an extensive general blacksmithing industry, in which he was associated with Peter Darling,
at the Muddy Brook water privilege, a " short distance south
from the highway that leads to Wainsocket."*

At the incorporation of the town of Cumberland, 1746, he
was chosen member of the town council, and filled other positions of public trust. Aug. 21, 1747, at a meeting of the
town, John Bartlett was chosen viewer of fences, in place of
Jacob, Jr., "moved out of town."† He and his wife, Lydia,
sold, March 30, 1758, their part of their deceased father
Muzzy's estate, situated on the Colony line in Mendon, to
Daniel Southwick.

Jacob, and his wife, Lydia, were members of the Society of
Friends—Quakers—and were married according to the peculiar method of that sect. He asked the society for a certifi-
cate of his appointment, 30: 7: 1731. He was delegated to
visit the quarterly meeting on Rhode Island, 29: 4: 1738; was
appointed to attend the marriage of Joseph Southwick and
Bethia Callum, 26: 2: 1739. He was appointed to settle differences between Hannah Comstock and James Muzzy, 30: 5:
1741. His intentions of marrige with Lydia Muzzy were made
known, 29: 8: 1742. With others, he was appointed, 27: 11:
1742, "to draw up something" concerning the keeping of slaves,
and " bring it to the next monthly meeting." He repaired the
meeting house at Providence, 29: 3: 1753. A complaint against
Jacob, by Daniel Bartlett, to the Preparative meeting, 27: 12:
1759, led to the appointment of a committee to examine the
merits of the case. This committee reported that " Jacob never
did make any covenant with Daniel relating to the complaint."‡
Jacob is often mentioned in the records of the Smithfield
monthly meeting, to which he belonged, and was repeatedly
chosen representative to the quarterly and monthly meetings.
A complaint was made against him 30: 9: 1762, for sitting

---

* The place in 1758 was owned and operated by Olney Burlingame.

† It does not appear to what place he removed. It is certain, however, that he was not far
away, and he may have been in Mendon.—T. L. B.] October 8, 1747, he sold to Charles Capron
15 acres, bounded north by the Woonsocket road; east, by the Rehoboth road, at the parting of
the roads, near his house, where he then dwelt, the property being bounded by Joseph Bartlett's land and the shoplot.

‡ This trouble, probably, grew out of the legacy which his uncle, Moses, left him, and it
caused much coarseness of accord. Jacob was obliged to bring a suit against Joshua Hall, the
executor of the will of Moses, before he could recover the £1279 which his uncle left him. The
Court, Dec., 1759, awarded him the full amount, together with the costs of the action.

with his hat on during prayers, and a committee was appointed to "labor" with him. The committee made a report
at the next monthly meeting, and presented a paper in writing
from said Jacob. The case was laid over until the next
monthly meeting, at which it was again referred to the next
meeting, as the paper he sent "was not satisfactory to the
meeting." At the ensuing meeting it was once more referred,
and for several successive monthly meetings the matter was
brought up and deferred, until it appeared to be dropped
altogether, as no mention of the disposal of the case finally
was subsequently made.

Jacob Bartlett, blacksmith and farmer, appears to have been
an excellent man in all that constitutes a good citizen and
exemplary Christian. He died, April 17, 1768, and was,
probably, interred in the old Bartlett burying ground. Lydia,
his wife, died Nov. 10, 1786.

In his will, made Nov. 19, 1760, he gives his daughter,
Amey Cass, his "Pewter, etc.;" to his son, David, his wearing apparel, except the cloak, which was his uncle Moses'; to
his daughter, Sarah, beds, bedding, etc., and to his wife,
Lydia, whom he made his sole executrix, all the rest of his
estate, money and otherwise. The will is recorded in Cumberland.

CHILDREN

(Of Jacob, Jr.)

AMEY, b. —— ; m. —— Cass.
DAVID, b. ——
SARAH, b. ——. She was published to Anthony Razee, of Cum-
berland, April 12, 1790.

> [I have no further account of this family. It may be that
> David went to Maine. There is a tradition that one of the
> family, in the early time, was a wealthy captain "down east."
> —T. E. B.]

(14.) JOSEPH BARTLETT[3] (*Jacob*[2]; *John*[1]).

Married Abigail Aldrich, Nov. 7, 1744, William Arnold,
Justice of the Peace, officiating. His father, Jacob, gave him,
6th Feb., 1737–8, his homestead, and two other tracts of land

already described—see Jacob². The 1st of March, 1745-6, his uncle, Moses, gave him his homestead, where the latter then dwelt, consisting of forty acres, etc., "about a mile from said town of Providence, bounded by the Killingly road, and the Plainfield road, at the parting of the two roads," etc., with all the buildings. He was admitted a freeman of Providence, May 1746. He appears not to have been more prospered on the estate than had been his brother, Jacob, who had previously had an experience there, and, May, 25, 1748, he sold, for £500, the same land to Moses which the latter had formerly given him, and returned to Bellingham and Cumberland,* and lived without further change, so far as ascertained, on the old homestead given him by his father, Jacob. This place, owned, in 1879, by George Waterman, and before referred to, is situated in the lot, a short distance west from the Mendon road, not far from the school house, where the old Boston turnpike, as it was formerly denominated, intersects with it, and is at about an equal distance from the Woonsocket road, on the south, and the residence of Joseph's son, Livin, now owned by Leprelet Miller.

The homestead house stands on a little knoll, facing the south, the barn being a few rods to the westward, and just back from the house, is the old well-sweep, where the "old oaken bucket" is still suspended, and seems to invite the thirsty pilgrim to partake of the clear, sparkling water in the well beneath, and over which it seems to hang, like a protecting arm. Near the well, is a large elm tree, under which, no doubt, several generations of the Bartletts have refreshed themselves, and been shielded from the hot rays of the sun in midsummer, by its widely spreading branches and thick foliage. About half way between the house and the Woonsocket road, is the old Bartlett burying ground, where a number of the generations of the Bartlett's have found rest, very near the scenes of their labors.

Between the house and the Mendon road, on the east side, stands the house that was occupied by Joseph's son, Joseph,

---

*The boundary line between the states had then been settled, and the old homestead was thereafter to be in Cumberland. Some of the land, however, was across the line, in Bellingham, the line dividing the land about an eighth of a mile north of the house.

Jr. It was owned, 1879, by Alexander Bartlett, a lineal descendant.*

Joseph, and his wife, Abigail, were Quakers, and members of the Smithfield Monthly Meeting. They were married in that society, and Joseph was frequently called upon to serve the society in different concerns. He was a member of the town council, and identified with the town's interests in various affairs. He was interested in the blacksmithing establishment on Muddy Brook, although confined principally to farming. It is handed down by their descendants that Joseph and his wife were a very pious couple, and took great pains with the education of their children in the ways of religion. Joseph was of a rather poetical turn of mind, and composed several poems, among which is one entitled, "A Father's Exhortation to his Children," and another, "To Such as are at Ease in Their Sins." He died, Dec. 1, 1791. His sons, Jacob and Abner, were administrators of his estate. Abigail, his wife, died about 1804. Both were buried in the old Bartlett burying ground.

Many persons have been eulogized for their great and good deeds, yet few have improved their opportunities as well, and left behind them such an enviable reputation for probity of conduct and purity of mind, as is accredited to the good, earnest, pious old Quaker—Joseph Bartlett.

CHILDREN
(Of Joseph and Abigail (*Aldrich*) Bartlett).

25. EBER, b. Sept. 7, 1745; m. Zibiah Razee.

ABEL, b. April 18, 1748; m. Sarah Callum, dau. of Daniel and Lydia Callum, of Mendon, Mass., July 3, 1788. He may have been married previously. He bought of Uriah Alverson, of Smithfield, March 4, 1785, land lying a part in Cumberland, and a part in Bellingham, on the north of Joseph Bartlett's land, and on the west side of the Mendon road. He and his wife were Quakers, and belonged to the Smithfield Monthly Meeting. They, probably, had no children. He d. Nov. 14, 1789, and his widow m. Daniel, son of Daniel and Mercy Smith, of Smithfield, June 7, 1798. Abel made his will, 29th Oct., 1789, and mentions his four brothers, Jacob, Abner, Joseph, and Livin.

CHLOE, b. Aug. 4, 1749; m. John Southwick, of Mendon, Mass., 1766. He was b. July 6, 1744, and d. Jan. 23, 1831. She d. April 25, 1817. Both belonged to the Uxbridge Monthly

Meeting. They had eleven children, namely: *Lucy*, b. April 22, 1767; *Eber*, b. Nov. 27, 1768; *Philadelphia*, b. April 5, 1770; *John*, b. Aug. 29, 1771; *Enoch*, b. June 7, 1776; *Amasa*, b. March 5, 1778; *Chloe*, b. Dec. 14, 1779; *Wait*, b. Jan. 10, 1782; *George*, b. Feb. 28, 1784; *Letitia*, b. Jan. 26, 1786; *Daniel*, b. Nov. 11, 1791. All lived to marry and settle in life.

26.   JACOB, b. Feb. 24, 1751; m. first, Judah Cook; second, Anna Cook. Went to Danby, Vt.

27   ABNER, b. April 9, 1752; m. Drusilla Smith. Went to Danby, Vt.
PHEBE, b. May 9, 1756; m. Jeremy Inman, and had *Nancy*, who d. young; *Lydia* d. æt. 15; *Sina* m. Stephen Jillson; *Abigail* m. Nathan Aldrich; *Joannah* m. Jonathan Sweet (brother of Anthony Sweet, who m. Maria, dau. of Bini Bartlett). *Joannah* was born June 21, 1792. She and her husband, Jonathan Sweet, have had seven children. He is dead, but she is still living (1879), and residing with her daughter, Caroline, in Cumberland. She was still quite smart, and with her memory unimpaired. [To her I am indebted for much information concerning these families.] She d. June 8, 1881, of old age.

28.   JOSEPH, b. Nov. 9, 1758; m. first, Phebe Sayles; second, Elizabeth Earl; third, Amey Clemens, who outlived him.

29.   LEVIN, b. May 6, 1763; m. Nancy Gaskell.

(15.) JOHN BARTLETT[4] (*Job*[3]; *John*[2]; *John*[1]).

He was born May 13, 1734; m. Deborah Phillips, Feb. 29, 1756. He was admitted a freeman of Cumberland, 1756. His homestead was at Manville, it being the same that fell to him from his father Job. He was an eminent physician, with a large practice. He was appointed Surgeon and Brigade Director of the Rhode Island Hospital, 1776, and was promoted to the rank of Surgeon General and served through the Revolutionary war. He was administrator of his father's estate. Job, his father, was no exception to the rule that lawyers seldom make correct wills, and, although in his lifetime he had made many binding instruments for others, his own will was not admitted to probate, and owing to some legal defect, was declared void. His son, John, being the eldest, was declared the legal heir to his estate. But John did not avail himself of this technicality. He carried out the provisions of the will, and gave his brothers and sisters just what the will allowed them, and what his father wanted them to have.* He died Dec. 14, 1784, and his wife was appointed guardian of John and Freelove, who were under age.

CHILDREN.

30   DANIEL, b. April 11, 1756; m. Phebe Arnold, dau. of Jacob Arnold, of Smithfield, May 22, 1782.
31.   ASA, b. Sept. 2, 1757.
      MARY, b. March 31, 1759.
      LEMUEL, b. July 31, 1761.
      FREELOVE, b. Oct. 13, 1771; m. James Lovett, Jr., of Mendon, Sept. 6, 1794.
      JOHN, b. March 27, 1776.

(16)   JOB BARTLETT[1] (Job[3]; John[2]; John[1]).

Born June 9, 1744, in Cumberland ; m. Oct. 29, 1775, Molly (daughter of Moses,) Ramsdell, of Mendon. He was an ardent patriot during the Revolution, and was actively engaged in raising troops.

CHILDREN.

32.   BENJAMIN; b. June 29, 1776; m. Mary Tucker.
33.   ELIJAH, b. April 3, 1778; m. Sally Bartlett, dau. of Asa Bartlett. She was b. Aug. 18, 1784. Both were of Cumberland. The marriage took place Sept. 17, 1807. He d. June 24, 1863, æt 85 years and 3 mos., of old age.
      JOHN, b. March 10, 1780.
      LEMUEL, b. April 26, 1782.
      JOANNAH, b. Oct. 19, 1785.

(17.)   JEREMIAH BARTLETT[1] (Jeremiah[3]; John[2]; John[1]).

He was b. Aug. 16, 1741 ; m., March 25, 1762, Rebecca Lapham, Justice of the Peace Nathaniel Cook officiating. Lived in Cumberland, and, during the American Revolution,

---

*Rarely in these more modern days, when the dollar appears to overcome the natural tendencies of consanguinity, is there a case of similar disinterested action on the part of one member of a family to another. Men like John Bartlett are not readily found among persons having business with probate courts.—T. E. B.

he manufactured cannon at Unity Furnace, Manville, for the use of the colony. One of the daughters married a Mr. Newman, and one of them married a Mr. Jeffers.

CHILDREN.

JOANNAH, b. Sept. 20, 1762.

MARCY, b. June 20, 1764.

REBECCAH, b. Nov. 15, 1766; probably m. Silas Clark. Several children.

ZEPHANIAH, b. Sept. 26, 1768. He lived in Cumberland, and had a son, Amos, and, probably, other children. Amos, in 1887, was living in Webster, Mass., aged about 89.

PRISCILLA, b. Jan. 12, 1771.

RACHAEL, b. May 28, 1773.

34. JEREMIAH, } twins; b. April 6, 1775.
SUSANNAH, }

Jeremiah m. Jerusha Jeffers, May 22, 1796, and went to Harmar, Ohio, 1805.

35. AMOS, b. March 17, 1777. Went to Harmar, Ohio, 1803.

LEVI, b. July 26, 1779; m. Hannah (daughter of Caleb) Jeffers, of Cumberland, Nov. 28, 1798.

(18.) RICHARD BARTLETT[1] (*Ezra[3]*; *John[2]*; *John[1]*).

He was b. Feb. 28, 1738; m. Keziah ——. According to the Killingly, Conn. records, Richard, of Gloucester, R. I., July 19, 1784, bought of Royal and Jonathan Mathewson, of Scituate, four tracts of land in Killingly, consisting of 180 acres, with all the buildings, etc.; April 3, 1785, he bought 80 acres on the "Rhode Island line," on the "Chestnut Hill road that leads to Providence." He bought, Dec. 19, 1785, from Richard Tucker, land in Killingly; also, June 1, 1794, he bought of Andrew Brown, of Killingly, a saw and grist mill; also, of Peltiah Mason, June 20, 1797, more land, and he had numerous other transactions in real estate at different times. He probably lived at Chestnut Hill, a short time, and apparently removed to Killingly about 1782. On the farm once owned by him are three cotton factories and their villages, containing seven or eight hundred souls. The house which he built still stands, in the center of the place, and in it five generations of the Bartletts have lived.[*]

CHILDREN.

SARAH, b, May 8, 1763; m. Nathan (son of Thomas Burlingame,) May 13, 1782.

BERTHA, b. Feb. 27, 1765; m. —— Taft.

LUCRETIA, b. March 27, 1767; m. —— Mitchell.

SUSANNAH, b. May 24, 1769; m. —— Seamans.

RICHARD, b. Nov. 10, 1771.

JEREMIAH, b. ——; m. —— Smith.

EALEZER, b. ——.

REUBEN, b. ——; m. Polly (daughter of Gideon) Burgess before 1800 [*see Burgess Genealogy*], and had a son, Waldo, and others. Waldo has a son, Henry W. Bartlett, living in Putnam, Conn.

(19.) NOAH BARTLETT[1] *Noah[3]; Samuel[2]; John[1]*).

Born March 9, 1723; m. Elizabeth Phillips, of Smithfield, July 14, 1776. He bought the farm of Edward Salisbury, March 28, 1771.

CHILDREN.

MARY, b. ——; m. Walter (son of Job) Phettaplace, May 15, 1792.

(20.) ISRAEL BARTLETT[1] (*Noah[3]; Samuel[2]; John[1]*).

He was b. April 5, 1737; m, Caroline Balcom, Nov. 12, 1781. He was guardian of his mother, who, after his father's death, became delirious. He asked the council to relieve him, 1763, as he was going eastward.[†] Removed to Mt. Desert, Me., probably, about 1785. He was a soldier in the French war, and served as lieutenant and captain during the Revolutionary war.

CHILDREN.

MARY, b. April 19, 1783; d. ——, æt. 82.

POLLY, b. ——, 1785.

NANCY b. ——, d. ——, æt. 79.

PHILA, b. ——, d. ——, æt. 81.

[*]Edward Bartlett, of Killingly, bought land in Killingly, 1797. Perhaps he was a son of Richard.—T. E. B.

[†*Cumberland records.*]

(21.) JEHO BARTLETT[4]; (*Noah*[3]; *Samuel*[2]; *John*[1]).

He was b. in Cumberland, June 16, 1739 ; m. Sarah Had-way, Sept. 13, 1761. Removed from Cumberland, R. I. to the south part of Sutton, Mass., about 1780. He d. Nov. 16, 1794.

CHILDREN.

BILOTHA, b. Feb. 11, 1762; m. Lieut. Jonathan Burden, of Sutton, Nov. 21, 1782. He was going across the fields to give information of the death of his brother-in-law, Ensign Bartlett, who had been crushed by falling under the wheels of his cart, and, it is supposed, fell backward as he was getting over the fence, and was killed by the fall, May 8, 1817. [*History of Sutton, Mass.*]

PHINEHAS, b. April 12, 1763, m. Kezinah —— and removed with his father to Sutton, 1780. He, or his father, Jeho, owned the place where George C. Allen now (1879) lives. He sold it to John Allen, who came from Holley, Vt., and probably removed to Boylstone, Mass. He may have had a second wife, Eunice, and may have lived in Holden. He left Boylestone 1801, and went to Ohio, where he died.

LILLIES, b. May 27, 1766; m. Elijah Sibley of Sutton, Nov. 21, 1822.

SARAH, b. March 19, 1768.

SQUIRE, b. Jan. 26, 1770.

ISRAEL, b. July 25, 1773.

THANKFUL HOPE,
MARY,
} twins; b. March 26, 1776.

HENRIETTA, b. June 10, 1777.

36. JOHN H., b. Nov. 18, 1779 ; m. Hannah Marsh, May 15, 1803. He was an Ensign, and d. May 5, 1817.

(22.) RUFUS BARTLETT[4] (*Abner*[3]; *Jacob*[2]; *John*[1]).

He was born in Gloucester, R. I., Nov. 16, 1739 ; m. Margret Smith. He soon removed to Cumberland, where he was a tavern keeper, carried on blacksmithing, and was surveyor of highways, etc. He was appointed by the Legislature in 1776, to raise arms for the town of Cumberland. He, together with Jonathan Holman, of Sutton, bought from John Dale, Aug. 5, 1779, ninety acres of land at Diamond Hill, with the

privilege of one-quarter part of all the iron ore dug up on
the land, the other three-quarters to belong to Dale, together
with all the privileges necessary to carry on the mining business.   He d. June, 1798.   She d. March, 1794, æt 60.

CHILDREN.*

ANNIE, b. Sept. 19, 1763; m. George Ballou, of Cumberland,
Sept. 12, 1794.†

ALPHA, b. Sept. 8, 1764; m. Whipple A. Lovett.

PHILADELPHIA, b. Jan. 7, 1766; m. Dr. Lamb, of Grafton, Mass.

MARY, b. Aug. 7, 1767; d. young, June 10, 1770.

ABNER, b. Sept. 17, 1771.

NATHAN, b. ——.

37.   SMITH, b. April 21, 1780.

RUFUS, b. ——; d. Jan. 24, 1779, in his 3d year.   His grave in the
old burying ground at Manville, R. I., is marked by a stone.

POLLY, b——; d. Feb. 1, 1785.   Her grave-stone is in the burying
ground at Manville.

(23.)   ELISHA BARTLETT¹ (*Abner³; Jacob²; John¹*).

He was b. in Gloucester, R. I., Sept. 7, 1742; m. Ruth,
dau. of Stephen and Ruth Arnold, of Smithfield, Sept. 25,
1769.   He was appointed, 1780, to raise recruits for Gloucester.   In 1787, was assistant to the Governor.   He had laid
out to him by the " Proprietors" of Providence, Sept. 9, 1771,
" 14½ acres within the grand purchase of Providence," described as situated on the west side of the " seven-mile line,"
and adjoining the farm which he then lived on.   He bought,
"at a place called the Fork, where the Branch runs into the
Pawtucket River," and also three-quarters of an acre of land
at the Branch bridge, and situated on the " north side of the
highway and running down stream, commencing at the bridge,
together with the stream of water and all the privileges
thereof."   It was here that Abner, his father, owned land, and
several of the Bartletts had previously bought and sold.‡   The

---

* Annie, Alpha, Philadelphia and Mary are recorded as born in Gloucester. The others
are recorded in Cumberland.

† (Ballou Genealo, v.)

‡ This place has always been known by the name of "The Branch."

water privilege was extensive, and Elisha, and afterward his son Otis, carried on a very extensive business, making scythes and edge tools, greatly to their pecuniary advantage. The old homestead house where Elisha lived is still standing on the east side of the road, a little south from the bridge, and by the side of it, quite a spacious one of more modern construction, probably built by Otis, and within which his son, Dr. Elisha, was born and died. During the time Dr. Elisha resided on the premises, he had a very fine nursery of fruit trees, etc., and two large peach orchards, which he caused to be set out on the place, were marvelous objects for that community.

The writer has very pleasant recollections of his boyhood on several occasions, at that place, with the enjoyment of the delicious peaches which grew there. None have since seemed so palatable, years having dulled the keen sense of youthful taste.

Investigation has not been thorough as to the first of the Bartletts who had possession of this water privilege, and it is very probable that it was here where the first John had his "half of grist mill and five acres of land adjoining on the Providence side," which is mentioned in his inventory, 1684. The mills and the rights in the stream are now (1879) owned by the Blackstone company, and Jerome Howard owns the farm and two houses, the older one of which in 1879, was unoccupied. The date of Elisha's death was not ascertained. His wife, Ruth, died Feb. 25, 1784.

CHILDREN.

ALPHA, b. Dec. 2, 1771; m. Caleb Aldrich.
PATIENCE, Dec. 5, 1773; m. Daniel Jenks, and had *Henry*, *Mary*, *Amelia*, *Sarah*, *George*, *John* and a *girl*. [*History of Woonsocket*.]
MARY, b. April 15, 1776, m. Comstock Passamore, and had *George*, *William*, *Joannah*, *John*, *Elizabeth*, and *Otis*.
38. OTIS, } twins, m. 1st, Waity Bullum; 2d, Waity Allen.
    OLIVER, } twins, m. Sarah Howe.
GEORGE, b. ——.
ABBEY, b. ——.
ABIGAIL, b. ——; d. Jan. 25, 1784, in her 2d year. [*Grave-stone.*]

(24.) CALEB BARTLETT[4] (*Abner*[3]; *Jacob*[2]; *John*[1]).

He was b. Jan. 19, 1745, in Gloucester ; m. Susannah, dau. of James Wilson, March 21, 1773. He was a farmer, and resided in what is now Burrillville, a town taken from Gloucester and incorporated Oct. 29, 1806, its name being in honor of Hon. James Burrill.

Caleb made his will Jan. 15, 1801, and died four days afterward. His brother, Elisha, was administrator of the estate. His children are all mentioned in the will, except Benedict and Ruth, probably not at that time living.

CHILDREN.

WILLIAM, b. Nov. 3, 1774.
ESTHER, b. Feb. 6, 1777.
JAMES, b. ——.
30. STEPHEN, b. ——; m. Lavina Sayles.
LUCY, b. ——; m., April 10, 1823, Luke, Jr., son of Luke and Sarah Aldrich, of Mendon. She d. Feb. 6, 1859, æt 68 years, 24 days. He died August 16, 1867, æt 87 years, 4 mos. and 25 days. Their memorial stones are in the Quaker burying ground, Smithfield. They were Quakers and were married in that Society.
POLLY, b. ——.
RUFUS, b. ——.
JAMES, b. ——.
BENEDICT, b. ——.
RUTH, b. ——.
PHILADELPHIA, b. ——.

(25.) EBER BARTLETT[4] (*Joseph*[3]; *Jacob*[2]; *John*[1]).

He was b. in Cumberland, Sept. 7, 1745 ; m., Jan. 6, 1771, Zibiah Razee, who was b. Oct. 13, 1746, and died about 1821–22. She was dau. of David Razee and his wife Freelove. Eber and wife were joined in matrimony by Nathaniel Cook. After marriage, Eber lived awhile with his father, Joseph, and built the house which stands on the east side of the Mendon road, directly opposite the Woonsocket road where it leads out of the Mendon road. The house and farm are now occupied by Miss Alpha Bartlett, dau. of Eber's son, David. Eber died at this house in the bedroom next to the road. During his sickness, which was brief, he was most of the time delirious.

He is described as of medium height, very finely built and very active and gentlemanly. After his death, his wife, Zibiah, removed to the log house which stood near the present residence of William I. Follet,* on the new road to Diamond Hill from Woonsocket, and lived there some years and worked at tailoring and maintained herself and four children, the oldest only ten years of age and the youngest only nine months, at the time of the death of her husband, Eber. It is said of her that she was one of the best tailors in those parts, and all who could secure her services considered themselves very fortunate. She is described as being very straight and unusually smart and afraid of nothing. It will not be doubted that she was smart. Had she not been so, she could not have brought up and educated her children in the excellent manner she did. In old age she was kindly cared for by her son, Bani, with whom she lived until death.

The date of Zibiah's death is not known. She was buried in the burying ground, opposite the old Elder Ballou meeting house, on the lot purchased by her son, Bani, and her grave is closely contiguous to his. Eber died Sept. 13, 1781, at 36 years and 6 days, and was buried in the "old Bartlett burying ground," near the homestead place of his father, Joseph

CHILDREN

(Of Eber and Zibiah (Razee) Bartlett.)

40. DAVID, b. Aug. 3, 1771; m. Hannah Joslyn.
41. BANI, b. Dec. 19, 1772; m. Philadelphia Pickering.
  CHLOE, b. April 21, 1777; m. Reuben Cook.‡
  SALOMA, b. Dec. 18, 1780; never married. She was a typical old maid of excessive neatness, and had a great fondness for buff color in dress, always wearing something of that color. She was a favorite with children, and was of a kind, benevolent disposition. She died at her brother, Bani's, house, on the new Woonsocket and Diamond Hill road, June 30, 1836, in in her 56th year,‡ and is buried in the Elder Ballou meeting house burying ground. In person, Saloma was of a tall, erect figure, and her manners were in accordance with her amiable temper and good heart.

*The house in which William I. Follet was living as recently as 1778, was built by Eber's son, Bani, near where the first log house stood.

†Reuben Cook was a well-educated man. Before marriage, he taught school some. He and his wife removed to Belchertown, Mass. They have had six or seven children.

‡The grave-stone says, "57th year,"—a mistake.

(26.)   JACOB BARTLETT[1] (*Joseph[3]; Jacob[2]; John[1]*).

He was b. Feb. 24, 1751, in Cumberland, R. I.; m., 1st, Judah
Cook ; 2d, Anna Cook, both wives being daughters of Samuel
Cook, of Smithfield, R. I. [*Cumberland records.*] For the
account of the Danby families, I am largely indebted to N. L.
Baker, Esq., of that town. He married Sophronia, dau. of
Jacob's son, Joseph ; there are also some extracts from the
Vermont Historical Gazetteer.

Jacob and his brother, Abner, removed from Cumberland
to Danby about 1795. They settled near the present homestead of Willard Baker, in Danby. Jacob's house was near
the old road, now discontinued. He was a Quaker. He was
the first one in the town to carry on blacksmithing ; this he
followed many years. Some of the work done in his establishment in 1797, is still to be seen. He died in Granville,
N. Y., Jan. 14, 1837, æt 86. His wife, Anna, died in 1846,
æt 96.

CHILDREN.
(By first wife.)

JEMIMA, b. ——.
ANNA, b. ——; m. Augustus Rogers. Settled in Ferrisburg, Vt.
NAOMI, b. ——; m. Albert Mead. Settled in Ferrisburg, Vt.
SARAH, b. ——; m. Richard Barnes. Lives in Saratoga, N. Y.
GEORGE, b. ——; d. young.

(By second wife.)

JUDITH, b. May 28, 1788; m. Enoch Colvin. Settled in Danby, Vt.
JACOB C. (5), b. July 5, 1789; m. Cynthia (dau. of Deliverance and
    Judith) Rogers, Nov. 2, 1815. She d. July 12, 1871. He died
    Aug. 24, 1873. They had only one child, *Anson* (6). [See
    Anson's descendants below.]
42. JOSEPH, b. Aug. 2, 1791; d. in 1876, æt 85.
DANIEL, b. Feb. 11, 1794; m. Eliza Potter.

ANSON BARTLETT[6] (*Jacob C.[5]; Jacob[4]; Joseph[3]; Jacob[2];
                John[1]*).

Anson Bartlett, the only child of Jacob C. Bartlett, was
b. in Danby, Vt., Oct. 21, 1816 ; m. Esther (dau. of John and
Levina) Rogers, also of Danby, Oct. 31, 1837. In 1838, he
removed to Munson, Geauga County, Ohio, where he purchased land and resided many years. In 1875, he located in

Collinwood, Ohio, where he died, May 29, 1891, in the 75th
year of his age. The funeral services, which were attended
by a large number of his neighbors, friends, and fellow townsmen, were very impressive, being conducted by the Masonic
fraternity, of which he was a member. The *Collinwood Times*,
of June 4, 1891, contained a worthy tribute to Mr. Bartlett's
memory. His blameless and honorable life was rich in usefulness to his fellow men. In early life he was engaged in
agricultural pursuits. He was the inventor of numerous ap-
pliances used in making cheese by machinery, and was the
first in the State to engage in this industry by the factory
process. He was President of the Ohio Dairymen's Association, and Vice-President of the National Association. He
frequently lectured in different parts of Ohio, and New York,
in the interests of the farming communities. He was for
twelve years the county surveyor of Geauga County. After
his death, his remains were taken to Munson, where they are
interred in the Maple Hill Cemetery.

CHILDREN

(Of Anson Bartlett.)

JOHN R., b. June 5, 1839, d. Aug. 21, 1839.

MARCUS, b. June 26, 1841, d. Aug. 1, 1841.

SILAS R., b. Sept. 28, 1842; m. Martha A. Hodges, Aug. 11, 1862,
    had seven children, viz.—*Minnie Eliza*, b. Aug. 7, 1863, d.
    June, 1870; *Jacob Clarke*, b. June 27, 1865, m. Ida Battles, has
    one son, Gordon Merl; *John R.*, b. July 27, 1867; *Esther M.*,
    b. Jan. 10, 1869, m. Edward Middleton and has one child
    living. Minnie A., b. May 11, 1885; *Cynthia Eve Ett.*, b. Dec.
    17, 1870; *Anna M.*, b. Aug. 15, 1873 d. June, 1879; *Jay S.*,
    b. Sept. 15, 1875.

MARY R., b. Jan. 10, 1844, m. William Hansard, Feb. 13, 1864.
    She died Dec. 27, 1864, and left one child, *Mary R.*

JOHN J., b. March 12, 1846, d. Sept. 6, 1846.

ELLEN, b. May 6, 1847, d. June 16, 1847.

NANCY, b. July 5, 1849, d. Sept. 30, 1849.

LUCIUS ANSON, b. Aug. 16, 1850; m. Angeline Corning, Jan 4,
    1871, and had *Idah Ruth*, Nov. 26, 1871; *Grace J.*, Feb. 3,
    1873; *Dwight C.*, May 13, 1876; *Mary J.*, Aug. 3, 1881;
    Hattie, July 19, 1883.

EVE ETT*, b. Aug. 11, 1854; m. Forrest O. Snow, Feb. 25, 1875.
    She has one child, *Roger D.*, b. Nov. 22, 1879.

ESTHER MALLIE, b. Jan. 7, 1859, d. Dec. 13, 1865.

*To Mrs. Eve Ett (Bartlett) Snow, Secretary of the Bartlett Reunion Association, I am
indebted for the account of the descendants of Jacob C. Bartlett and his son, Anson. She resides in Collinwood, Ohio.—T. E. B.

(27.) ABNER BARTLETT[1] (*Joseph[3]; Jacob[2]; John[1]*).

He was b. in Cumberland, R. I., April 9, 1752 ; m. Drusilla, (dau. of John) Smith, of Smithfield, Sept. 27, 1781. Both were Quakers. He removed to Danby, Vt., about 1795. Soon after, his brother Jacob, went thither. The following year, he built a house on the hill, east of Nelson Kelly's, which is still standing. He died, 1801. The births of all the children except Jeremy, are recorded in Cumberland, R. I.

CHILDREN.

DEXTER, b. Sept. 22, 1782 ; m. Rachael, (dau. of Jonathan) Staples. He inherited his father's homestead. Removed to Holland Purchase, N Y., in 1840, and died there, 1866.

AMEY, b. July 12, 1784 ; m. Levi Taft.

43.   SAVID, b. Nov. 5, 1787 ; m. Prusia Allen.

SMITH, b. April 11, 1790 ; m. Sally Allen.

44.   ABEL, b. June 25, 1793 ; m. Hannah Boomer.

LYDIA, } twins ; b. April 25, 1795.
MARY, }

45.   DANIEL, b. April 8, 1798 ; m. Ruth Rogers.

JEREMY, b. 1800 ; m. Rhoda, (dau. of Stephen) Wheeler, and settled on the Prince Allen farm, Danby, Vt. He succeeded his brother Abel, after Abel's death in 1821, in manufacturing scythes, hoes, rakes and other implements, at the old establishment. Here, the first trip-hammer in town was constructed by Savid Bartlett and Isaac Southwick, near the residence of Henry B. Kelly, in 1810. Jeremy removed to Collins, N. Y., in 1845. He died 1867, æt 67.

(28.) JOSEPH BARTLETT, JR.[4] (*Joseph[3]; Jacob[2]; John[1]*).

Was b. Nov. 9, 1758, in Cumberland, R. I.; m. 1st, Phebe Sayles, of Smithfield, by whom all his children were born. She died about 1810, and was buried in the Bartlett burying ground, south of the old house. He m. 2d, Widow Elizabeth Earl, of Leicester, Mass. Her name before marriage was Chase, and she was a sister of Job Chase. She lived a few years and was buried in the Quaker burying ground, at Smithfield. He then m. 3d, Amey, (dau. of Richard and Amey) Clemens, of Smithfield, Oct. 9, 1822. They were married in the Friends' meeting-house, in Burrillville, the wedding reception taking place at the house of Buffum Chase, which stands on the Batty farm, and where Amey made her home. She was a woman of good abilities and had a kind, amiable disposition and was an excellent step-mother.

In stature, Joseph was of medium height and rather slender; of light complexion. His manners were engaging. He was noted for a benevolent and truly Christian character, and he had no enemies that were ever heard of—every one liked " Uncle Jose," as he was called ; for he had a pleasant word for all. He was one of the genuine sort of Quakers who always give four pecks to the bushel. He lived in the house owned, in 1878, by Alexander Bartlett, a great grand-son, situated between the old homestead and the Mendon road, and which was built for him by his father, Joseph. During the few latter years of his life, he was very feeble and troubled with trembling so much that he was almost helpless. He died September 12, 1835, æt 76, and was buried on the Hill, northwest of the house. His wife, Amey, lived until February 4, 1849, dying in her seventy-eighth year. She is buried by the side of her husband.

CHILDREN.

46. EBER, b. Feb. 19, 1785; m. Patience Scott.
47. ELISHA, b. July 29, 1786; m. Martha Inman.
48. BRINTON, b. March 19, 1788; m. Bula Jillson.
     PHEBE, b. June 21, 1793; m. Chad Mason, and had only one child,
        a daughter.
     STEPHEN, b. May 30, 1795; never married.
     NAOMI, b. June 23, 1797; never married.
     SYLVIA, b. April 26, 1799; d. Sept. 6, 1847, in her 49th year. She
        was buried on the hill where her father's remains lie. She
        never married.

(29.) LIVIN BARTLETT[4] (*Joseph*[3]; *Jacob*[2]; *John*[1]).

He was b. May 6, 1763, in Cumberland, R. I.; m. Nancy (dau. of William) Gaskill, Feb. 18, 1786. He lived on the Woonsocket road and had a good farm. His land abutted that of his father, Joseph, on the north, and a drive-way connected the two places. His house and farm are now owned by Leprelet Miller. Uncle Livin, as he was called, was a very diligent attendant at the Friends', or Quakers' meeting, although he did not belong to that society.

In stature, he was not quite of medium height, and rather spare. He was not much of a talker, but still, quiet, and unobtrusive in habit, and was respected as an honest, upright man. He died, ——, and was buried in the old Bartlett burying ground, between his house and his father Joseph's. His wife is also buried there, together with his sons, Lemuel and Livin, Jr.

CHILDREN.

PHILA, b. April 15, 1786.
49. GEORGE, b. Sept. 2, 1789; m. Nancy Cook.
LEMUEL, b. Dec. 22, 1791: no issue.
NANCY, b. Jan. 12, 1804; m. —— Bourn. Some descendants live
    in Providence, R. I.
LIVIN, b. Dec. 2, 1806; no children.

(30.) DANIEL BARTLETT[5] (*John[1]; Job[3]; John[2]; John[1]*).

He was b. April 11, 1756, in Cumberland, R. I.; m. Phebe (dau. of Jacob) Arnold, of Smithfield, May 22, 1782.

CHILDREN.

WILLIAM, b. Nov. 24, 1782.
SUSANNAH, b. June 9, 1784.
DANIEL, b. July 10, 1786.
LEMUEL, b. April 1, 1788.
RHOBY, b. Nov. 10, 1789.
DEBORAH, b. Jan. 8, 1792.
ROWENA, b. Feb. 7, 1794.
POLLY, b. Dec. 31, 1797.

(31.) ASA BARTLETT[5] (*John[1]; Job[3]; John[2]; John[1]*).

Born in Cumberland, R. I., Sept. 2, 1757; m. Patuna ——. He was a farmer, and owned a part of the first cotton factory built at Manville, R. I. He always lived at, or near, Manville.

CHILDREN.

SALLY, b. Aug. 15, 1784; m. Elijah (son of Job) Bartlett.
ALPHA, b. May 3, 1788; was 2d wife of Elijah Bartlett, her sister
    Sally's husband.
JAMES, b. Nov. 23, 1790.

(32) BENJAMIN BARTLETT⁵ (*Job⁴; Job³; John²; John¹*).

He was born June 29, 1776; m. Mary (dau. of Morris) Tucker, Feb. 5, 1797. Both were born in Cumberland, R. I.

CHILDREN.

BENJAMIN, b. July 28, 1798; d. March 13, 1858.
JOB, b. Sept. 4, 1801.
MARY ANN, b. Dec. 22, 1802.

(33) ELIJAH BARTLETT⁵ (*Job⁴; Job³; John²; John¹*).

He was b. April 3, 1778; m. Sally (dau. of Asa) Bartlett. She was b. Aug. 18, 1781. He died of old age, June 24, 1863, æt 85 years and 3 months. His and his wife's parents were of Cumberland. Elijah m., 2d, Alpha, b. May 3, 1778. She was sister of his first wife.

CHILDREN
(By first wife.)

50. ARNOLD, b. about 1805; m. Sally Beebe.* He d. in Cumberland, 1830. She d. in Smithfield, 1845.
WILLIAM, b. Aug. 12, 1812; m. Rosina Arnold, April 7, 1845. They had *Nathan Arnold*, b. Feb. 12, 1847; m. Bridget Doherty, Feb. 21, 1871. *George Francis*, b. Jan. 19, 1872; d. young. *William Herbert*, b. Jan. 9, 1874; d. young. [*Ballou Genealogy.*]

(By second wife.)

ALVIN, b. ——; m. Amey Ann (dau. of Patience and Elkhannah) Whipple. She d. in Cumberland, Aug. 11, 1859, æt 48. He d. about 1831-2. Their children were *George* and *Otis*, who live in Attleboro, Mass., *Ira*, who lives in Woonsocket, R. I., and a daughter, *Abby*. The three sons have children.

(34) JEREMIAH⁵ (*Jeremiah⁴; Jeremiah³; John²; John¹*).

He was b. in Cumberland, R. I., April 6, 1775; was a twin brother of Susannah. He m. Jerusha, dau. of Caleb and Jerusha (Dyer) Jeffers, May 22, 1796. She was b. in Cumberland, Nov. 8, 1776. I am indebted to Dr. J. C. Bartlett, of Marietta, Ohio, a grandson, for the following interesting account of them and their descendants.

*Sally Beebe was dau. of Mrs. Grace Beebe, b. 1782, whose father, George C. Claghorn, was builder of the United States frigate, Constitution.

Jeremiah went with his family to Harmar, Ohio, in the fall of 1805, his brother, Amos, having preceded him. He bought land of the Ohio Company's survey, about three miles above Harmar, on the left bank of the Muskingum. After building a house, he took his family there in the fall of 1806. In 1813, he bought eighty acres of land, in Wesley township, Washington County, Ohio, near what is now Bartlett Post Office. While at this place, he was taken sick, but was able to be about the house until until the day he died in 1813. He was buried in the Harmar burying ground, near the center of the plot. He was a strong man, five feet, nine inches high, and weighed one hundred and eighty pounds. His wife, Jerusha, was of medium size, strong and sprightly. She d. April 20, 1868, at the house of her son, Levi, whose farm included the land first bought by his father at Harmar, in 1806. She was buried by the side of her husband.

CHILDREN.

LIVA*, b. May 14, 1797, in Cumberland, R. I.; m. in Marietta, Ohio, Jan. 30, 1817, Robert Gibson, b. in Westmoreland County, Pennsylvania, March 7, 1793. Both d. in Delaware County, Ohio. Liva in April, 1838, and he, May 10, 1866. They had twelve children: *George, Mary, John, Eliza, Lucinda, Levi, William, Minerva, David, Luther, Calvin, Abigail.*

PERSILLA, b. Nov. 11, 1798, in Cumberland, R. I.; d. at the home of her brother, Levi, in Harmar, Jan. 4, 1875.

51. SMITH, b. March 22, 1800; in Cumberland, R. I., m. June 19, 1825, Mary Willis.

ANNA, b. Dec. 1, 1801; m. in Harmar, Sept. 2, 1830, William P. Olney. He d. at Dubuque, Iowa. She was living in 1880, at Delaware, Ohio.

MARIUM, b. Oct. 31, 1803; d. on the farm above Harmar, July 18, 1826.

52. LEVI, b. July 20, 1805; m. Maria Dickey, Oct. 26, 1837; m. 2d, Nov. 11, 1851, Phebe, (dau. of Ezekiel Canfield,) a widow of Leonard Greene.

FEARING, b. June 22, 1807; d. at the farm, June 2, 1825.

SUSAN, b. Jan. 1, 1810; m. Feb. 14, 1828, John Roop. He d. They had, *Emeline* and *John.* She m. 2d, June 9, 1851, her cousin, Amos Bartlett, and had two more children. [*See Amos No. 53.*]

MARY, b. March 9, 1812; m. in Harmar, June 1, 1852, Moses Rardine, P. O., Brown's Mills, Washington Co., Ohio.

JEREMIAH, b. May 20, 1814; d. Oct. 15, 1814.

*Recorded in Cumberland, R. I.—" Elvira."

(35.) AMOS BARTLETT[5] (*Jeremiah*[4]; *Jeremiah*[3]; *John*[2]; *John*[1]).

He was b. in Cumberland, R. I., March 17, 1777. He was tall, of sallow complexion, quiet in deportment, and had a good faculty for business and money making. He was a tanner. Went to Harmar, Ohio, in 1803, and on the bank of the Muskingum, directly opposite the foot of Washington street, Marietta (then a stockade fort), built a house and tannery. The house (1880), with additions, is in good repair, *i. e.*, the first story, which is of stone. In 1811, he sold the property and went to Parkersburg, Va. (now West Virginia), where he also carried on business as a tanner until his death, from pulmonary disease, Sept. 29, 1815. He was buried in the Harmar, Ohio, burying ground, by the side of his brother, Jeremiah. The horizontal sandstone slab, with its inscription nearly obliterated, was, in 1880, well fixed in its place, and a large sycamore tree encroaches upon the grave at its foot. He m. in Harmar, Ohio, Sept. 16, 1806, Mary Reardin. She m. again after his death.

CHILDREN.

HANNAH, b. July 20, 1807, in Harmar, Ohio; m. Dec. 17, 1829, Alexander Randal. They went to Iowa about 1840. They had *Selinda, Elizabeth, Andrew, Amos, Caroline*. In 1875, Andrew and Amos were living near Peoria, Mahaska County, Iowa.

SELINDA, b. Aug. 13, 1809, in Harmar; m., May 24, 1824, James Petty. They went to Iowa about 1840. They had *James Alexander, Clementine* (who m. James Samuels), *Mary* (m. David Boyd), *Rebecka J.* (m. James Redpath), *Amos D., Lucy* (m. Thomas Bubel), *Gifford H., Francis Iowa* (m. Davidson), *Royal Haden*, all of whom were living, in 1875, near Peoria, Mahaska County, Iowa.

53.   AMOS, b. July 16, 1812, in Harmar, Ohio; m., Nov. 15, 1830, Elizabeth Garrard. Went to Iowa in 1840; m., 2d, his cousin, Susan Roop, widow, a dau. of his uncle, Jeremiah Bartlett.

JACOB, b. June 16, 1814, in Parkersburg, W. Va.; m. in Washington County, Ohio, April 25, 1837, Margaret Rubel. They went to Iowa. They had four children, *Susan, Lucy, Selinda* and *Owen*, who, in 1874, was in Yankton, Dakota.

(36.) JOHN H. BARTLETT⁵ (*John*⁴; *Noah*³; *Samuel*²; *John*¹).

He was b. in Cumberland, R. I., Nov. 18, 1779. His father removed to the south part of Sutton, Mass., the year after the child's birth. He m. Hannah Marsh, May 15, 1803; d. May 5, 1817, his death being caused by falling in front of his heavily loaded cart, the wheel of which passed over his head, crushing it in a horrible manner. His wife, Hannah, died at Uxbridge, Mass., April 23, 1815.

CHILDREN.

> CYNTHIA, b. April 8, 1804.
> LUCINA, b. April 15, 1809.
> PHINEHAS, b. Oct. 17, 1811.

(37.) SMITH BARTLETT⁵ (*Rufus*⁴; *Abner*³; *Jacob*²; *John*¹).

He was born in Cumberland, R. I., April 21, 1780; m. Nancy (dau. of John) Russell. She was born in Providence, R. I., July 17, 1782, and d. at Kingston in the Dominion of Canada, Feb. 11, 1819.* John Russell, her father, was in the fifth generation from John Russell, Sr., who settled in Woburn, Mass., about 1640. Smith Bartlett m., 2d, Mrs. Sarah Gladding, widow of Benjamin Gladding, sister of his first wife. The latter was born in Providence, R. I., May 22, 1780, and died at Cape Vincent, Oct. 4, 1851. Smith Bartlett d. at Cape Vincent, Jefferson County, N. Y., Nov. 11, 1867, in his 87th year. He was a merchant, and removed to Canada in 1806.

CHILDREN.

> WILLIAM RUSSELL, b. Dec. 7, 1803; in Providence.
> JOHN RUSSELL, b. Oct. 23, 1805, in Providence, R. I. He was a distinguished author, and member of various learned societies; was appointed by President Zachary Taylor to fix the boundary line between Mexico and the United States. He was Secretary of State of Rhode Island seventeen years. He d. in Providence, R. I., May 28, 1886.
> SMITH, JR., b. May 13, 1808; d Aug. 22, 1868.
> MARTHA RUSSELL, b. June 6, 1810; d. Oct. 24, 1865.
> GEORGE FRANCIS, b. Aug. 23, 1812.
> ROBERT COLEMAN, b. May 10, 1815; d. Dec. 15, 1853.

---

*The Upper Canada *Herald*, at her death, paid a glowing tribute to her memory. The funeral sermon was preached by Rev. Alexander Fletcher, and was printed at Kingston. For a full account of the family of Smith Bartlett, all the members of which were very eminent, two sons of John Russell Bartlett at present holding commissions in the United States Navy, see the *Russell Genealogy*, by Hon. John R. Bartlett.

(38.) OTIS BARTLETT[5] (*Elisha[4]; Abner[3]; Jacob[2]; John[1]*).

Born Feb. 20, 1778, in Smithfield, R. I. (Branch Village.) Married, 1st, Waity (dau. of William) Buffum; m., 2d, Waity (dau. of Mehitable and Walter) Allen, Sept. 7, 1826. Waity Buffum was b. Sept. 29, 1783. Waity Allen was b. May 9, 1793. Otis carried on the scythe manufacture and a farm at the Branch Village. He and both wives were Quakers, members of the Smithfield Monthly Meeting. He was in stature of medium height and rather spare. He was possessed of the perseverance and industrious habits characteristic of the Bartletts, and was influential in the community.

CHILDREN.

(By first wife.)

ELISHA,[*] b. Oct. 6, 1804; graduated from Brown University, receiving the degree of M. D., in 1826; m. Elizabeth (dau. of John) Slater. He d. July 15, 1855. A distinguished author and physician. He was a professor in various colleges, and was elected Mayor of Lowell, Mass.

CAROLINE, b. March 11, 1806; m. I. Brown, of Providence, R. I.

ADELIA, b. Jan 1, 1808.

REBECCA, b. Sept. 1, 1810; m. J. D. Brown, of Providence, R. I.

RUTH, b. June 14, 1812.

OLIVER, b. Oct. 17, 1815.

GEORGE, b. Sept. 23, 1817.

WILLIAM OSBORN, b. April 3, 1820.

SARAH EARLE, b. Aug. 28, 1822.

(By second wife.)

WALTER OTIS, b. Oct. 18, 1836.

(39) STEPHEN BARTLETT[5] (*Caleb[4]; Abner[3]; Jacob[2]; John[1]*).

Born in Burrillville, R. I.; m. Lavina Sayles. His homestead was on the old Burrillville road, about two miles from Slatersville. He was an extensive farmer, and also carried on blacksmithing. He was a large, well-proportioned man of portly

---

[*]Dr. Elisha inherited his father's property at the Branch. I have no record of any children.—T. E. B.

and commanding appearance. His son, Elisha, in 1879, was living on the old place.

CHILDREN.

PHILADELPHIA, b. ——; m William H. Andrews, of Woonsocket, R. I. They lived on the Globe side.

MINERVA, b. ——; never married.

ELISHA (6), b. May 30, 1808; m. Sarah Ballou (b. Feb. 15, 1810), July, 3, 1831. They had *Atwell* (7), b. Dec. 22, 1833; m., Sept. 3, 1853, Caroline Elizabeth Ballou, who was b. Nov. 24, 1833, in Burrillville, R. I. *Sophia Louisa*, b. Oct. 2, 1835; m. Benjamin Joslyn. *Fayette Earl* (7), m. H. F. Reynolds, Oct. 26, 1865.*

ATWELL BARTLETT[7] (*Elisha*[6]; *Stephen*[5]; *Caleb*[4]; *Abner*[3]; *Jacob*[2]; *John*[1]).

Born in Burrillville, R. I., Dec. 22, 1833 ; d. Feb. 17, 1871, æt 37 years, 1 month, 26 days.

CHILDREN.

ERWIN ATWELL, b. Feb. 13, 1855.
ADFER, b. Dec. 21, 1861.
GEORGE ELISHA, b. Dec. 27, 1863.
SARAH LAVINA, b. Dec. 25, 1868.

FAYETTE EARL BARTLETT[7] (*Elisha*[6]; *Stephen*[5]; *Caleb*[4]; *Abner*[3]; *Jacob*[2]; *John*[1]).

Born in Burrillville, R. I., Nov. 12, 1840; m. H. F. Reynolds, Oct. 26, 1865.

CHILDREN.

FRANCIS FAYETTE, b. April 29, 1867; d. young.
SOPHIA LOUISA, b. Nov. 14, 1868.
MARION DELCINA, b. Jan. 10, 1870.
WALDO REYNOLDS, b. May 2, 1874.
MARCELLA MINERVA, b. Aug. 8, 1877.

(40.) DAVID BARTLETT[5] (*Eber*[4]; *Joseph*[3]; *Jacob*[2]; *John*[1]).

Born Aug. 3, 1771, in Cumberland, R. I.; m. Hannah Joslyn, at Warren, R. I., Aug 25, 1798. They lived awhile in the Zebina Cook house, which stood a little distance in the rear of the present (1879) residence of Darwin Cook. Afterwards, when his brother, Bani, had built a new residence and had removed thither, he moved into that house which was vacated by Bani, and where he, David and his wife, Hannah, died, and which is now owned and occupied by his daughter, Miss Alpha Bartlett. This was the house where his father, Eber, lived and died, and it stands opposite the intersection of the old Woonsocket road with the Mendon and Providence road.

In appearance and stature, David was large and portly, and of very engaging manners. He held many positions of trust in the town government, and was several years High Sheriff of the County of Providence, during which time he and his family lived in Providence. He was for many years one of the "deputies," and was considered a good business man and successful farmer. He d. Sept. 3, 1842, æt 71 years, 1 month, and was buried where lie his wife and son, in a small inclosure a few rods west, on the opposite side of the stream from the shop now owned by Olney Burlingame. His wife d. May 11, 1852, æt 79 years, 7 months. They had only two children, neither of the latter having married.

CHILDREN.

ALPHA, b. Nov. 30, 1795; single. Was living as recently as 1879.
SETH, b. March 17, 1802. He was drowned, Dec. 4, 1842, by breaking through the ice on Peter's River, while returning from Woonsocket.

(41.) BANI BARTLETT⁵ (*Eber*⁴; *Joseph*³; *Jacob*²; *John*¹).

Born in Cumberland, R. I., Dec. 19, 1772; m. Philadelphia Pickering (youngest dau. of Samuel* and Sarah (Ballou) Pickering, of Bellingham, Mass.), Jan. 27, 1802 (pub. Dec. 6, 1801).

*Samuel Pickering was a near relative of the patriot, Timothy Pickering, and died May 31, 1807, æt 72 years, 2 months. His wife (Sarah Ballou) was one of the first members of the "Elder Ballou Church" in Cumberland. They lived in Bellingham, on the Mendon and Providence road, just south of the present New York and New England railroad. The house and farm are now owned by Asel Mann. It was in this house that Philadelphia was born, and in which she was married to Bani Bartlett. Mr. Pickering bought land from Samuel Scott, on the Mendon line, Sept. 22, 1758, he being then of Mendon. He was published to Sarah Ballou, of Bellingham, Nov. 21, 1758. Their children were: *Rosanna*, b. Dec. 5, 1759, published to Ahab Arnold, Sept. 24, 1780; *Sarah*, b. Feb. ——, pub. to Anthony Razee, of Cumberland, April 13, 1787; *Simeon*, b. July 20, 1761, published to Rhoda Wilson, Feb. 10, 1788; *Mary*, b. Aug. 3, 1765, *Asenath*, b. Dec. 8, 1768; *Esther*, b. April 29, 1772, published to William Billings, July 13, 1789; *Ruth*, b. Sept. 23, 1774; *Bernice*, b. June 29, 1777; *Philadelphia*, b. Oct. 31, 1779, m. Bani Bartlett, Jan. 27, 1802.

She was b. Oct. 31, 1779. They lived awhile with her parents in Bellingham, until he built his house on the hill. This house was then situated some distance from the road, and was approached by a drive-way which led by Nathaniel Jillson's, but when the new road from Woonsocket to Diamond Hill was made, the road was laid out close to the house. This house is on the north side of the new road and about one-half mile east from where it crosses the "old Mendon road." The land at this place belonged to his father, Eber, and was inherited by Bani. It was here that the log house stood, in which his mother, Zibiah, lived, after becoming widowed. The cellar excavation where it stood could be seen a few years ago and its location quite clearly defined, but these marks have now disappeared and it would be difficult to fix its location precisely, although it stood about five or six rods north from the present highway and on the upper side (east) of the present house and about the same distance from it.

After living here a while, he rented this place and occupied his father's old house and farm on the Mendon road (where Alpha Bartlett now lives at the junction of the Woonsocket road) and, beside carrying on the farm, he built a dam across the brook, just below the house, and erected a scythe shop,[*] quite a large one for those days, and carried on the business of manufacturing scythes, sending them to Boston, Worcester, Providence, and other places for a market, and also to the neighboring towns. All of his boys assisted him in some department of the industry, and they all learned the practical details of scythe-making. The following autograph was taken from a bill of sale of scythes sold in Worcester, 1829:

Bani Bartlett

After living here many years, he gave up his manufacturing, and his brother, David, took the house and farm, and he went back to live on his old place,[†] on the hill, where he and his

[*] This shop has long since gone to decay, and there is not much to show where it stood. A portion of the dam can be made out and also the place where the shop stood. There is much less water in this brook than formerly, and it is now used for a watering place where it crosses the road. The shop stood by the side of the road at this watering place and on the north side of the brook.

[†] William Follet owned the place in 1880.

wife died. In stature, Bani was above medium height, very straight and of excellent proportions, and was spoken of generally as being a very handsome man. His complexion was rather light, and in his advanced years he was quite bald on his head.

His wife was of medium height, rather dark complexion, fair and plump, and had beautiful dark eyes, and was of very charming appearance and of a delightful disposition. She was a loving mother and a real helpmate as a wife, being gifted with unusual qualities of heart and mind. Her quickness of perception and remakable activity, united with a sympathetic nature, made her presence a pleasure wherever she went, and she had the admiration and love of all who knew her. She d. April 4, 1837, in her 58th year, and is buried by the side of her husband in the " Elder Ballou" burying ground, where Bani had purchased a lot and caused his mother, Zibiah, to be buried after her death.

Bani was a man of few words and of very even disposition, and in his intercourse with others was characterized by his firmness and dignity and good sense. He was always self-possessed and never allowed himself to exhibit passion or feeling, and it is said of him, and his wife, that there was never heard an unkind or a scolding, harsh expression, escape from the lips of either.

He was for more than twenty years Deputy Sheriff of Providence County, and in the performance of the delicate duties connected with that office, he probably made as few enemies as would have been possible for any one to have done. And the few old people who remember him, speak of him as a man who was universally respected in the community where he lived. His name frequently appears on record in connection with the settlement of deceased persons' estates, and he was often appointed administrator, a circumstance which indicates the great business capacity he was known to possess, as well as attests the general confidence and esteem in which he was held by his friends and neighbors. He died July 24, 1835, in his 63d year, his death being caused by the use of the water which came to the house through a lead pipe. He is buried by the side of his wife, and mother, in the "Elder

Ballou" burying ground. From the road, and facing the burial
place, his lot is on the right-hand side, about half way across
the ground and is next to the driveway, and wall, which extend
around the grounds. In approaching his lot from the road,
the first grave is that of his mother, Zibiah. At its head and
foot are rough memorial stones, having no inscription. The
next grave by its side has a plain, unpretending stone, in-
scribed as follows :

"IN MEMORY OF
MR.
BANI BARTLETT,
WHO DIED
JULY 24, 1835,
IN HIS 63D YEAR."

The third grave, and by the side of the grave of Bani, is
that of his wife,[*] the inscription on the stone reading :

"IN MEMORY OF
MRS.
PHILADELPHIA,
WIFE OF
BANI BARTLETT,
WHO DIED
APRIL 4, 1837.
IN HER 56TH YEAR."

The next and fourth grave, by the side of that of his mother,
is that of Eber, son of Bani, and on the granite headstone is
cut the following :

"EBER BARTLETT,
SON OF BANI
AND
PHILADELPHIA,
BORN
SEPT. 18, 1805.
DIED
JAN. 6, 1876."

If the date of her birth as recorded in the *Bellingham Records* is correct, she was in her
58th year at the time of her death.

There is a vacant space—room for one more grave—and then comes the little grave of Edwin S., infant son of Bani's daughter, Sarah, who married George Tingley. Next to this, the grave of the mother, Sarah, who died July 4, 1841, in her 34th year. The next, and on the other side of the grave of the mother, is that of her little daughter, Phila, æt 2 months and 15 days. The next and last grave in the family lot is that of Bani's sister, Saloma, who died June 30, 1836, in her 57th year.

CHILDREN

(Of Bani and Philadelphia (Pickering) Bartlett.)

WILLARD, b. Oct. 22, 1802; d. Dec. 6, 1809. He was buried in the "Old Bartlett Burying Ground."

MARIA, b. April 20, 1804. She was of the same lovely disposition that characterized her sister's. She m. Anthony Sweet,* of Cumberland, Aug. 18, 1825. They have lived in Blackstone, Mass., many years. He died there. She, in 1879, was still living. They had nine children, viz: *Sterry*, b. June 28, 1826; m. Carry Sweet, a cousin of his uncle, Burrill Bartlett's wife. They have lived many years in Olneyville, R. I. They had five children. *Andrew Jackson*, b. July 14, 1828; named by his grandfather, Bani Bartlett. Lived many years in Providence, R. I. He m. Cordelia Hewet, and had three children. She died some years ago. *Sarah Maria*, b. Feb. 1, 1830; m. —— Martin, and went to Vermont and died there. They had six children. *Elizabeth*, b. Oct. 6, 1832; m. —— Martin, brother of her sister, Sarah's, husband. Went to Vermont and died there. They had three children. *Ellen*, b. Dec. 1, 1834, m. Jerome Bolster, of Uxbridge. They lived in Blackstone, and had two children. She is living, a widow. *Richard*, b. April 16, 1837; m. Mary ——, and lives in Ashton, R. I., where he was postmaster and merchant. He had two boys. *Marsella*, b. Feb. 10, 1840; m. —— Talbot, and lives at Norwood, near Boston. He is a farmer. They have had one child, if not more. *Hannah*, b. April 18, 1843; m. William Cates. They live in Blackstone, and have two children. *Marianna*, b. Oct. 22, 1845. Was the first wife of her sister, Hannah's, husband, William Cates. She died soon after her marriage.

54 EBER, b. Sept. 18, 1805; m. Deborah Brownell.

SARAH, b. Feb. 29, 1808. Sally, as she was called, m. George Tingley, of Cumberland, a farmer. They had two children, who died young. She was of a lovely Christian character and a great favorite, and was very much beloved by all the family. She d. July 4, 1841, in her 34th year, firm in the belief of a

*Anthony Sweet was a brother of Sylvester Jillson's mother. Sylvester Jillson's second wife was Maria's sister, Lavina Bartlett.

blessed immortality.* George Tingley m., second, Nancy Jillson, first cousin of Anthony Sweet, who m. Maria, sister of Sarah Bartlett. Both were living in 1879. He is a wealthy and respected farmer, and resides at Diamond Hill, where he owns a beautiful residence and fine farm.

VARNUM, b. May 10, 1810; never married. He owned his father's farm on the hill and carried it on for a time. Afterward, he engaged in the boot and shoe business at Blackstone, Mass., and carried it on there many years. He lived with his sister, Maria, and died at her house. He was of quiet, modest habits, and was greatly respected by all who knew him. He d. Aug. 14, 1871, and was buried in the cemetery at Blackstone.

LAVINA, b. June 16, 1814; m. Sylvester W. Jillson,† Feb. 18, 1857. She was his second wife. They lived at Warwick, Mass., where he owns a farm. Lavina has had no children. Before her marriage, she taught school and, like her sister, Sally, early espoused the cause of religion, and has invariably been esteemed for her benevolent disposition and consistent Christian character. She has always been deeply interested in the Sunday school, and the good seed sown by her in the faithful service of her Master has fructified for her reward, for she frequently saw it spring up and bear fruit, and "future generations will rise up and call her blessed."

55. BURRILL, b. Oct. 22, 1816; m. Ann (dau. of Asel) Phettaplace, of Greenville, R. I.

(42) JOSEPH BARTLETT⁵ (*Jacob¹; Joseph³; Jacob²; John¹*).

Born in Rhode Island, probably in Cumberland, and when about three years of age, went with his father to Danby, Vt. His first wife was Pheby (dau. of Stephen) Colvin. She d. 1823, æt 29, and he m his brother, Daniel's, widow, whose maiden name was Eliza Potter. He m., third, Mary (widow of Phillips) Potter, dau. of Ebenezer Smith. She was but three years younger than he and outlived him. He was over eighty when he died in 1876. He retained his great mental and physical vigor with little impairment to the end of his life. He was during all his career a very industrious, active man, and resided all his life in Danby. He was a natural and ingenious mechanic, and built a great many houses, much of

*Buried in the Elder Ballou Burying Ground.

†Sylvester Jillson's first wife was Mary (dau. of Jonathan) Kendall, of Hubbardstown, Sic d. March 14, 1856. He was a chair manufacturer in Gardner, Mass., until 1851, when he removed to Warwick. By his first wife, he had *Justus, Henry* and *Emma*. Justus was for some years State Superintendent of Schools in South Carolina, and was finely educated. Henry is in South Carolina, and holds office in the U. S. Internal Revenue department.

his work being done by "Scribe Rule." In 1812, he was drafted to serve in that war. In 1827, he built the saw mill known as Brown's Mill, and in 1837, the grist mill now owned by H. B. Jenks. He was very quiet and domestic in habits, and highly esteemed. All of his children have been church members.

CHILDREN.

MARY ANN, m. Joel Chamberlin, and removed to Ohio. Both are dead. They left three children (sons).

IRA, m. Huldah Colvin. Resides in Granville, N. Y., and is a a Quaker. He is a respected farmer. They have three daughters.

SOPHRONIA, m. Nathan L. Baker, of Danby, and settled on the David Griffith farm. He is a highly respected and influential citizen of Danby. They have had several children.

HENRY, m. Salusha Davis; m., second, the widow of Alfonso Willard. He lives in Chardon, Ohio. He began life farming and cattle dealing, but is now a merchant in Chardon. He is a member of the Campbellite church, and is very wealthy. He has seven children, among whom are two sons, *Charles*, of Utah Territory, a Morman, and *Marcus* who lives with his father.

(By second wife.)

DANIEL, m. Olive (dau. of Samuel) Emerson, and lives in Chagrin Falls, Ohio. Has three daughters.

PHEBE, m. Frank A. Carpenter, of Poultney, Vt. He left no children.

CHLOE, m. ——— Fuller, and resides in Ohio. Has had three sons and one daughter.

GEORGE, m. Sarah Jane Smith. He was killed at the battle of Pittsburgh Landing, in the Union service. Left a wife and one daughter.

(43.) DAVID BARTLETT⁵ (*Abner*¹; *Joseph*³; *Jacob*²; *John*¹).

Born Nov. 5, 1787, in Cumberland, R. I., and went with his father to Danby, Vt., when about seven years old. He m. Prusia (dau. of Prince) Allen. He became an enterprising and influential man and was a worthy citizen. He carried on the business of making machinery and edge tools. He built a trip-hammer in 1810, near the High bridge, for the manu- facture of edge tools, which business he conducted for more than thirty years, a blacksmith shop being operated in con-

nection with the manufactory. He was called, and sustained
the reputation of being, the manufacturer of the best scythes
in the country. Many of his scythes and axes are in existence. He was a selectman from 1821 to 1824, and filled
various positions of trust and honor. In 1840, he removed
with his family to Holland Purchase, N. Y. He d. in 1856.
His wife d. in 1868, in advanced years.

CHILDREN.

ABNER.
PRINCE.
RUTH.
SMITH.
DAVID.
MARCUS, m. Fanny (dau. of Azel Kelly. Settled in Danby, Vt., a
    while, being a professional school teacher. Was the first
    superintendent of public schools. Removed to Collins, N.
    Y., and was assistant assessor of internal revenue for the Gov-
    ernment, but in 1878, was living in Buffalo, N. Y.
PLVN, m. Susan (dau. of Ephraim) Chase. Lives in Collins, N. Y.
    He has on his place a valuable horse, brought from Danby. It
    is valued at $5,000.

(44)   ABEL BARTLETT[5]; (*Abner[4]; Joseph[3]; Jacob[2]; John[1]*).

Born in Cumberland, R. I., June 25, 1793, and went with
his father to Danby, Vt.; m. Hannah Boomer. He was a
blacksmith and worked in the shop with his brother, Savid.
He was burned to death in 1821, while burning a coal pit on
the farm now owned by Josiah Southwick. A cabin which
stood near the coal pit, and inside of which he was sleeping,
in company with two persons, caught fire, and before he
could escape, he inhaled the flame and survived only a short
time. He was about 27 years old at the time of his death.
His widow is living in Danby, with her daughter, Ann, and
is over eighty years of age. Abel and wife had two children.

CHILDREN.

ANN, never married.
ABEL, m. Mary McLaughlin and resides in Spuyten Duyvil,
    N. Y. He is inventor and patentee of several useful things,
    among which is the Bartlett Polar Refrigerator, extensively
    known. He is also a landscape painter and an artist of pure
    taste. He has acquired a large fortune. He has two children,
    Charles and *Ada*.

(45) DANIEL BARTLETT[5] (Abner[4]; Joseph[3]; Jacob[2]; John[1]).

Born April 8, 1798, in Danby, Vt; m., first, Ruth (dau. of Deliverance) Rogers; m., second, ——— ———, from Rhode Island. He represented the town in the Legislature several years following 1834, and was selectman a few years. His occupation was that of a farmer, and he owned a very large farm, on which he kept forty cows besides other stock. He was justice of the peace from 1825 to 1841, and a leading man in the town. After his second marriage, he went West and there died. Some of his children are living in Ohio at this time, 1878.

CHILDREN.

Lucius succeeded his cousin, Marcus, in the superintendency of schools.

WING.

JOHN.

DELIVERANCE.

MARY, m. Freeman Paddock, of West Dorset, Vt., and resides there.

LYDIA.

MARTIN.

DAVID.

REMARKS.

December, 1877, I received a lengthy, interesting letter from N. L. Baker, Esq., of Danby, Vt., a few points from which deserve attention. Mr. Baker is a wealthy and influential citizen of Danby, and married Sophronia (dau. of Joseph) Bartlett, son of (Jacob[4], Joseph[3], Jacob[2], John[1]). Mr. Baker kindly forwarded me a copy of the History of Danby, a book now very rare, and from it I have obtained some items of information respecting the descendants of Jacob and Abner, who migrated from Cumberland, R. I., to Danby, about 1795. Mr. Baker, in writing of the history, says :

" I think it quite a valuable and reliable book, and I do not know where I could get another. It is one father Bartlett owned, and the cover and binding are his own work, when he was seventy-eight years old." * * * " I have been acquainted with the families of Bartletts for fifty years and my wife has always lived in this town." * * * * " Our youngest son, Summner W., died in June, 1876. He was 18 years and 6 months

old when he died, and a boy of great promise. Our son, Henry
S., is now in River Falls, Wis. Our three girls are well
married, and we have no reason to complain. So we are left
without any children at home. Our son, Henry S., has been
County Superintendent of Schools in Pierce County, Wis.,
for two years and at the November election was elected for
two years more.* His salary is quite large. He owns a house
and an academy building, which he rents to a man who graduated at the same college with himself, (Middlebury College.)
He also holds a local preacher's license in the M. E. Church.
His wife is a daughter and only child of Samuel Williams of
that place, (formerly of Herkimer County, N. Y.") * * * * " A
few more items in regard to the Bartletts and I am done. There
is no male of the name now in town. As I stated at first, I
have known them many years, and I have never heard of a
single person, old or young, bearing the name of Bartlett, who
was ever concerned in any dishonorable or even unmanly act,
which is saying something for a name that is so widely known
in all this part of the country. At one time, nearly all these
Bartlett families were here. They were good citizens and
most of them great readers and men of intelligence and
greatly respected by their neighbors "

(46.)   EBER BARTLETT⁵; (*Joseph⁴*; *Joseph³*; *Jacob²*; *John¹*).

Born in Cumberland, R. I., Feb. 19, 1785 ; m. Patience,
(dau. of Samuel) Scott, of Bellingham, Mass., Nov. 27, 1810.
Was the inventor of one of the best cooking stoves of the
time. In the latter years of life, he was partially insane. His
wife was also insane and died in the hospital.

> MADISON, b. Sept. 8, 1811.
> JULIA ANN, b. May 26, 1813.
> EBER, b. Oct. 15, 1815.
> MARY, b. May 14, 1817.
> PATUNA, b. Sept. 19, 1820.
> SAMUEL, b. June 22, 1822.
> JOHN, b. Aug. 16, 1824.
> PHEBE, b. Dec. 16, 1825.

*He was first put up as an independent candidate and elected by a large majority over the
regular candidates of the two political parties.—T. E. B.

(47.) ELISHA BARTLETT⁵ (*Joseph*¹; *Joseph*³; *Jac b*²; *John*¹).

Born in Cumberland, R. I., July 29, 1786; m. Martha (dau. of Francis) Inman, of Cumberland, Feb 23, 1808 ; d. Feb. 5, 1849, æt 62, and is buried in a burial place situated on the Providence and Mendon road, nearly opposite the present residence of Richard Bartlett.

CHILDREN.

SUSANNAH, b. April 19, 1809; d. May 1, 1859, æt 50 years and 12 days. She is buried near her father on the Providence road.

PHILA, b. Sept. 4, 1810 ; m. Zebina Cook, Jr., his second wife, and had ten children. He had two by his first wife.

56. ABNER, b. Sept. 12, 1812 ; m. Lucina Esten.

LOUISA, b. ——; m. Warren White.

SARAH, b. ——; never married.

JOSEPH, b. ——; died single.

RICHARD, b——; m. Emeline Hall. He is a wealthy farmer and an influential citizen. He resides in the new town of Woonsocket, which was formerly a part of Cumberland, R. I.

DELIA, b. ——; m. Smith Saunders.

DRUSILLA, b. ——; never married.

HARRIET, b. ——; m. Gilbert Jillson.

WILLIAM, b. ——; m. Sarah Gordon. They had *Julia*, d. Nov. 6, 1858, æt 3 months. Perhaps other children.

(48.) BRINTON BARTLETT⁵; (*Joseph*¹; *Joseph*³; *Jacob*²; *John*¹).

He was born in Cumberland, R. I., March 19, 1788 ; m. Bula Jillson, Nov. 5, 1815.

CHILDREN.

WELCOME JILLSON, b. Feb. 6, 1819; m. Nancy Adams. They lived in Woonsocket and had only one child b. there. *Eldora Maria*, b. May 27, 1846 ; d. Sept. 6, 1847.

STEPHEN, b.

LEANDER, b.

—— ——, b. ——; m. ——Hamilton.

(49) GEORGE BARTLETT⁵; (*Livin⁴*; *Joseph³*; *Jacob²*; *John¹*).

Born in Cumberland, R. I., Sept. 2, 1789 ; m. Nancy, (dau. of Zebina and Prusia) Cook.

CHILDREN.

PHILA, b. Jan. 19, 1811 ; m. John White of Burrillville, R. I., and had *J. B. White*, still single, *Julia Ann*, and a child who died young.

GEORGE L., b., Nov. 22, 1813 ; m. O A. Bowen, b. May 9, 1817. They resided in Woonsocket. Had *William Lewis* and *Phebe Ann*. Both d. young

WELCOME C., b. Dec. 8, 1815 ; m. Amey A. Whipple. They had *Alonzo* who d. young, and *Willis*.

WILLIAM O., b. March 8, 1817 ; m. Caroline Bowen. They had *Ellen* and *William*.

STEPHEN, d. young. •

JULIA ANN, b. March 19, 1821; m. Seth A. Cook, (son of Seth,) of Mendon, Mass. They had one daughter, *Emma*.

HARVEY, b. Sept. 14, 1822; m., first, Dolly Smith ; second, Mrs. Sarah Hall. No issue. He lives in Connecticut.

SETH, b. Jan. 6, 1827. Single.

WILLIS, d. young.

FRANCIS, d. young.

(50.) ARNOLD BARTLETT⁶; (*Elijah⁵*; *Job⁴*; *Job³*; *John²*; *John¹*).

He was b. about 1805 ; m. Sally, (dau. of —— and Grace) Beebe. She d. in Smithfield, 1845. He d. in Cumberland, 1839. They had eight children.

CHILDREN.

HENRY ARNOLD, b. July 15, 1827, in Uxbridge, Mass. He m. Charlotte Grow, dau. of Russell Grow, of Westford, Vt. They reside in Philadelphia He has made a large fortune in the manufacture of blacking and other enterprises, and has a large establishment on North Front street, Philadelphia. He is an example of a self-made man. His two sons live at home, viz: *Henry Ashley*, b. in Milbury, Mass., 1849, and *Frank Arnold*, b. in Philadelphia, 1857.

CHANNING, S., b. Dec. 6, 1831, in Smithfield ; m. Mary Simmonds of Cumberland, R. I., Aug. 28, 1858. They lived (1858) in Providence, R. I., and have several children.

ERASTUS.

MARY.

HARRIET.

Three other children, the last six dying in infancy.

(51) SMITH BARTLETT[6]; (*Jeremiah*[5]; *Jeremiah*[4]; *Jeremiah*[3]; *John*[2]; *John*[1]).

Was b. March 22, 1800 in Cumberland, R. I.; m. in Washington County, Ohio, June 19, 1825, Mary Willis. She was b. May, 1800. At the time of their marriage, he bought land adjoining on the north side of that which his father bought in 1806, on the Muskingham river. On the farm, he reared a family of five children. After the death of his wife, January 27, 1867, he went to Harmar and lived with his son, John W., and d. there Nov. 18, 1870, and is buried by the side of his wife in the Harmar burying ground. The grave is directly south of that of his father and Uncle Amos.

CHILDREN.

LUCINDA, b. Sept. 12, 1825; m. June 8, 1845, James L. Wells, son of Hartness and Mary (Keepers) Wells, of Freehold, N. J. He died in New York City, Feb. 10, 1863. She d. in Harmar, Dec. 18, 1867. They had *John W.* and *Huldah*, who both reside in Moline, Ill.

JOHN W., b. Aug. 10, 1828; m. in Red Bank, N. J., Nov. 11, 1851, Sarah R. Dailey, b. Feb. 23, 1829, in Monmouth, N. J. They resided until 1871, in Harmar, when they removed to Nashville, Tenn. In 1873, they went to Moline, Ill., where they were living in 1880.

SARAH A., b. July 25, 1830, d. in Harmar, May 26, 1864. She m. Nov. 25, 1849, John Scott, b. June 13, 1826, in Harmar. They had *John D., Mary, Charles* and *William*.

HARRIET, b. Sept. ——, 1833; d. Sept. 29, 1852

SYLVESTER, b. March 8, 1838; m. in Harmar, Dec. 18, 1856, Louisa A. Mosholder. Their ten children were all born in Washington County, Ohio. Their address, in 1880, was Browns Mills, in the same county. Their children were: *Mary E.*, b. Nov. 11, 1857; *Lizzie M.*, b. Jan. 23, 1860; *Smith*, b. March 10, 1862, d. Sept. 15, 1863; *John S.*, b. June 13, 1864, d. Sept. 24, 1870; *Addie P.*, b. April 26, 1867; *Charles K.*, b. Jan. 8, 1871; *Nillie E.*, b. July 2, 1873; *Lillie L.* and *Linna* — twins—b. Nov. 10, 1875; *Georgiana*, b. Oct. 22, 1878.

(52.) LEVI BARTLETT[6] (*Jeremiah*[5]; *Jeremiah*[4]; *Jeremiah*[3]; *John*[2]; *John*[1]).

Was b. in Cumberland, R. I., July 20, 1805. Two months later, his parents started for Ohio, his mother carrying him on her lap on horseback most of the way, reaching Harmar late

in October. He was a strong, active man, five feet, nine
inches high, weighing about two hundred pounds. With his
love for books and study, he was prepared on reaching the
age of twenty, to take a country school, and for the next
twelve years was a teacher most of the time. He was county
surveyor, and in 1852, a Representative in the Legislature.
At the time of his death, he owned, including that bought by
his father in 1806, one of the finest farms in the state. He
was injured by being thrown from his buggy, his horse having
been frightened, and three days afterwards, May 18, 1879, he
died, and is buried in Oak Grove Cemetery, Marietta, Ohio.
He m. Maria Dickey, dau. of Solomon Dickey, Oct. 26, 1837.
She was b. in Harmar, Nov. 13, 1816, and d. at the Bartlett
farm, April 19, 1846, and is buried by the side of her husband in
Oak Grove Cemetery, Marietta. She was of medium size and
had a pleasant disposition. He m., second, Phebe, (dau. of
Ezekiel) Canfield, Nov. 11, 1851. She was the widow of
Leonard Gunn. Dr. J. C. Bartlett of Marietta, Ohio, has a
complete record of the descendants of Soloman Dickey, the
father, and John Dixon, the grandfather, of Maria Dickey.

CHILDREN.

JEREMIAH C., b. Sept. 23, 1838 ; m. Jan. 27, 1870, Mary F. Hart,
  b. in Harmar, Jan. 27, 1950, dau. of Dr. B. F. Hart* and
  Sally M. Alcock. He studied at the University of Ohio, at
  Athens ; graduated from the Medical College of Ohio at
  Cincinnati, March, 1865, and from the department of Medicine
  and of Analytical and Applied Chemistry, of the University of
  Michigan, 1868. He has an extensive practice, and is one of
  the most notable and skillful physicians in Marietta, Ohio.
  To him we are indebted for the full and interesting account of
  the descendants of Jeremiah and Amos, who migrated from
  Cumberland, R. I., to Ohio, in 1806.

ELIZA B., b. April 11, 1840 ; m. May 24, 1865, Newell D. Hayward,
  who was b. and d. in Waterford, Ohio. She was educated at
  Holbrook Normal School, Lebanon, Ohio, and since her
  husband's death in 1865, has been a teacher. In 1880, she was
  living in Charlestown, Mississippi County, Mo.

GEORGE W., b. Aug. 29, 1841, d. May 4, 1844. He is buried with
  his father, in Oak Grove Cemetery, Marietta.

HENRY C., b. July 21, 1843; was with the 63d Regiment, O. V. I.,
  from its formation. Was with it in all its engagements; carried

---

*For an account of this family, see Hart Genealogy, published by Austin Hart, New
Britain, Conn., 1875.

the regimental flag three years, was never absent from duty or sick. As his comrades expressed it, he was the bravest of the brave. He went to Georgetown, Colorado, in 1869 and in 1880, was living there.

WILLIAM, b. April 19, 1846, the day his mother d. In 1871, he went to Chillicotha, Livingston County, Mo., where he was in 1880. He m. April 1, 1875, Isabella F. Palmer, widow of A. A. Harper, in Lexington County. They had two children, *M. C.*, b. Sept. 8, 1876 and *Manda F.*, b. Nov. 18, 1877.

(By second wife.)

ELLA, b. Aug. 28, 1852; m. Sept. 15, 1875, Prof. W. H. Campbell. They were living in 1880, in Charleston, Mo., where he has charge of an Academy. They have *Harry B.* and *William C.*

DANIEL C., b. Feb. 23, 1854.

LEVI, b. Nov. 19, 1855.

ASA, b. Sept. 17, 1857.

ADDA A., b. Nov. 6, 1859.

ANNA M., b. May 24, 1862.

JENNIE P., b. Feb. 22, 1864.

NETTIE H., b. Feb. 27, 1866.

FRANK H., b. May 19, 1868.

(53.) AMOS BARTLETT[6] (*Amos[5]*; *Jeremiah[4]*; *Jeremiah[3]*; *John[2]*; *John[1]*).

Born in Harmar, Ohio, July 16, 1811; m. there, Nov. 18, 1830, Elizabeth Gerrard, b. 1815. They went to Iowa about 1840, where she died in Mahaska County, March 16, 1848. He m., second, at Harmar, June 9, 1851, Susan Roop, widow of John Roop, and daughter of his uncle, Jeremiah Bartlett. He d. at Pella, Mahaska County, Iowa, Oct. 11, 1873. She was living, in 1880, at Peoria, Mahaska County, Iowa.

CHILDREN.

ELIZABETH, b. Sept. 30, 1831, in Marietta, Ohio; m., in Mahaska County, Iowa, May 11, 1849, Allen B. Goodby, b. in Montgomery County, Ind., Feb. 17, 1825. They had nine children.

ANDREW J., b. Aug. 11, 1835, at Vinton County, Ohio; m. —— ——. His post office address in 1880 was Flint, Mahaska County, Iowa.

AMOS, b. Sept. 3, 1837, near McArthur, Vinton County, Iowa; m. in Mahaska County, Iowa, Sept. 20, 1860, Nancy A. Mitchell, b. in Beaver, Penn., Dec. 9, 1840. They had eight children, viz: *John M.*, b. Sept. 22, 1861; *James J.*, b. April 10, 1863; *Oliver S.*, b. Feb. 4, 1865, d. young; *William C.*, b.

Dec. 19, 1867; *Carry C.*, b. Oct. 28. 1870; *Harriet E.*, b. Oct. 22, 1872; *Roscoe*, b. June 14, 1876; *Monroe*, b. July 22, 1878; all b. in Iowa.

GEORGE, b. Oct. 15, 1839, near McArthur, Vinton County, Iowa; m., Sept. 5, 1867, Rachel Swisher, b. in Ohio, Oct. 29, 1849. They had five children, all b. in Adair and Mahaska Counties, Iowa, viz: *Joseph*, b. Sept. 17, 1868; *Alva*, b. April 2, 1870; *Catharine*, b. Dec. 29, 1872; *Nora*, b. March 28, 1875; *Viola*, b. June 8, 1877.

(By second wife).

WILLIAM, b. June 14, 1853, in Mahaska County, Iowa; m., in the same county, Dec. 4, 1873, Julia Nutter, b. in Harrison County, Va., Dec. 30, 1853. They had: *Ida*, b. Dec. 3, 1874, in Marion County, Iowa; *Charles*, b. Feb. 18, 1876, in Mahaska County, Iowa; *Daisy*, b. Aug. 9, 1878; *Charlton*, b. Aug. 31, 1879.

JEREMIAH, b. Jan. 31, 1854, in Mahaska County. Iowa; m., in the same county, March 10, 1878, Maria A. Short, b., in Tama County, Iowa, March 17, 1862.

(54)   EBER BARTLETT[6] (*Bani[5]; Eber[4]; Joseph[3]; Jacob[2]; John[1]*).

Born in Cumberland, R. I., Sept. 18, 1805; m., at Burrillville, R. I., Aug. 29, 1830, Deborah Brownell. She was b. Sept. 10, 1808, and d. Nov. 15, 1891. She was dau. of Shadrach Brownell, and grand-daughter of Thomas Brownell, of Westport, Mass. After their marriage, they lived near the Livin Bartlett homestead in Cumberland. While here, Eber was engaged in the manufacture of scythes, with his father. After a while, he removed to Laurel Ridge, Burrillville. R. I., and, under the firm name of Bartlett & Faxon, carried on an extensive business, manufacturing cotton warp. He afterwards lived for a time in Smithfield, R. I., on the place since known as the "Edward Hotchkiss farm," a short distance, southwest, of the Quaker meeting house. It was here their son, Thomas Edward, was born; their daughter being born while they lived in Burrillville. In the fall of 1848, he removed with his family to Fayette, Maine, where he was for some years engaged with R. B. Dunn, manufacturing scythes. While here, his two children, Thomas Edward, and Mary Elizabeth, attended school at the Maine Wesleyan Seminary, Kent's Hill, about a mile distant from Fayette. After return-

ing to Rhode Island, he finally settled in Providence, where
he d. Jan. 6, 1876, in the 71st year of his age. He is buried
in the Elder Ballou burying ground in Cumberland, by the side
of his mother. His father, aunt Saloma, sister Sarah, and
grandmother Zibiah, are buried in the same plot. He retained his youthful activity and vigor, almost unimpaired, to
the end of life. In stature, Eber Bartlett was about medium
height, erect, and well formed. He had fine, dark-brown hair,
dark eyes, light complexion, regular features, and a very fair,
clear skin, and was called a good-looking man. In disposition, he was warm-hearted, quick, and impulsive, and very
generous and sympathetic, always ready and willing, in sickness, or misfortune, to lend a helping hand. No one, in dis-
tress, ever applied to him in vain for counsel, or relief. He
was a zealous temperance advocate, and his faithful labors, in
this field of benevolence, for the benefit of his fellow men,
were productive of much good. Like his kinsman, the good,
and pious, old Quaker, Moses, of Providence, who, when he
sold land, stipulated, that there should never be any strong
drink sold on the premises, he never enquired whether it
would pay, or not, or stopped to count the cost, when con-
tending with the evils of intemperance. In his family, he was
the most kind, and affectionate of husbands, and the most
tender, and loving of parents ; no sacrifice was considered
by him too great to make for the benefit of his children.

> " *Thank God, for one dead friend,*
> *With face still radiant with the light of truth,*
> *Whose love comes laden with the news of youth,*
> *Through twenty years of death.*"

CHILDREN

(Of Eber and Deborah *(Bracewell)* Bartlett.

ELIJ RUSSELL, b. in Cumberland, R. I., Jan. 10, 1832; d. Sept.
13, 1832, æt nine months, in Fall River, while his parents were
there on a visit. He was buried at Apponogansett, about five
miles from New Bedford, Mass., in the Quaker burying
ground.

MARY ELIZABETH, b. Dec. 11, 1833, in Burrillville, R. I. She
taught school some years; m. George W. Nason, and lives in
Exeter, N. H. They have had no children.

57. THOMAS EDWARD, b. April 17, 1835, in Smithfield, R. I.; m.
Emeline O. Barbour, of Bellingham Mass.

(55.) BURRILL BARTLETT[6] (*Ban[5]*; *Eber[4]*; *Joseph[3]*; *Jacob[2]*; *John[1]*).

Born Oct. 22, 1816, the youngest child ; m. Ann Phetta-place, of Greenville, R. I., Feb. 20, 1845. For some years, he was engaged in the grocery trade, but finally established himself as a soap manufacturer on Friendship street, Provi-dence, R. I., under the firm name of Phettaplace & Bartlett, his wife's brother being of the firm. He has accumulated a large fortune ; has been honored by his townsmen with many offices of trust, both in the City and State governments, and was a member of the City Council many years. He has but two children, one a civil engineer and the other a whole-sale grocer.

CHILDREN.

LEWIS LELAND, b. March 27, 1848.
ASEL PHETTAPLACE, b. Nov. 14, 1852; m. Mary A. Palmer, Nov.
   1, 1876. He has one daughter, Florence, b. Aug. 1, 1877, and
   perhaps others.

(56.) ABNER BARTLETT[6] (*Elisha[5]*; *Joseph[4]*; *Joseph[3]*; *Jacob[2]*; *John[1]*).

Born Sept. 12, 1812, in Cumberland, R. I., and lived on the old Joseph Bartlett, Jr., place ; m. Lucina Esten, Jan. 1, 1834. She was b. Nov. 23, 1806, and lives at the same place with her son, Alfred E., who inherited his father's homestead, —Abner, the father, having died April 17, 1856, æt 44. He is buried in the small burial plot on the hill, northwest of the house.

CHILDREN.

58. ALFRED E., b. Aug. 12, 1836; m. Almeda S. Pickering.
    ALEXANDER M., b. Dec. 1, 1840.

Yours truly
Thomas Edward Bartlett

(57.) THOMAS EDWARD BARTLETT⁷ (*Eber⁶*; *Bani⁵*; *Eber⁴*; *Joseph³*; *Jacob²*; *John¹*).

Born in Smithfield, R. I., April 17, 1838 ; m. Emeline Orinda Barbour, in her father's house in Bellingham, Mass., Oct. 27, 1859, Rev. Mr. Macy officiating. She was b. July 15, 1837, and was the dau. of Adams J. Barbour, Sr.,* and his first wife, Orinda (*Arnold*) Barbour. They lived for a time after marriage in Providence, R. I., where he was in charge of one of the departments in the Providence Tool Co.'s armory. In 1865, he went to Ilion, N. Y., and was foreman and contractor for several years in the Remington Armory. Returning east in the fall of 1871, he engaged in the grocery and provision business at 727-29 Main street, Worcester, Mass., where he remained until 1878, when he removed to Cambridge, Mass., where he will reside during the time his son, Frederic Russell, is pursuing his studies in the Harvard University Medical School. He is at present (1880) in charge of the passenger transportation business of the Boston and Hingham Steamboat Co., in Boston. During his father's residence in Fayette, Me., he attended school at the Maine Wesleyan Seminary, Kent's Hill ; was also several years a student at the Quaker School, Providence. In stature, he is about six feet high, and weighs one hundred and eighty pounds ; has dark-brown hair and dark eyes. In tastes, he is strongly antiquarian ; is a corresponding member of the Worcester Society of Antiquity. Is a great reader, and highly values the use of books.

CHILDREN.

> FREDERICK RUSSELL, b. Sept. 10, 1860, at (old) No. 16, Fountain street, Providence, R. I. He graduated at the High School, Worcester, Mass., June, 1875, and was admitted, without conditions, to the Harvard University Medical School the same year. After completing his term of study in 1881, he attended the College of Physicians and Surgeons in Boston, Mass., and was graduated M. D., May 28, 1883. He m., June 17, 1882, at Milford, Mass., Hattie N., dau. of Jacob M. and Laura A. (Eldridge) Hill. He has one son, *Frederic Russell, Jr.*, b. Feb. 28, 1883, at Boston, Mass.

*Adams J. Barbour was a lineal descendant of Capt. George Barbour, one of the original proprietors of Dedham and Medfield, Mass.

(58.) ALFRED E. BARTLETT[7] (*Abner*[6]; *Elisha*[5]; *Joseph*[4]; *Jacob*[2]; *John*[1]).

Born Aug. 12, 1836, in Cumberland, R. I.; m. Almeda S. Pickering, March 27, 1859. She was b. Sept. 23, 1843. They live on the old Joseph Bartlett, Jr., place, and his mother, Lucina, lives with them. They are a very happy and prosperous family. It was gratifying to find that they had kept an accurate genealogy of their family for several generations.

CHILDREN.

HARRIET A., b. March 28, 1860.
HENRY W., b. Dec. 2, 1862.
HERBERT A., b. March 23, 1864; d. March 9, 1865.
HERMAN L., b. March 21, 1865; d. Sept. 16, 1865.
MALENA S., b. April 3, 1866.
ROSCO, b. March 23, 1868.

MISCELLANEOUS.

A few miscellaneous names of Bartletts which occur in the notes taken from the records in Cumberland and adjoining towns, their relationship to the others of the same name not having been established.

CUMBERLAND.

John S. Bartlett and wife, Lucy, had

CALISTA, b. March 4, 1822.
WILLIAM H., b. April 25, 1826.
JULIA ANN, b. April 13, 1828.

(By second wife, Sally.)

LYMAN A. S., b. March 28, 1844.
HORRACE S., b. Sept. 5, 1839
THOMAS W. D., b. Feb 16, 1848.

HARRIET P. BARTLETT, m. Gilbert L. Jillson, Oct. 24, 1847, both of Woonsocket, R. I. They resided in Douglass, Mass. She was b. Nov. 14, 1826. They have had seven children.

ABNER BARTLETT, wife, Susan, d. Jan. 29, 1807. *Smith J. C.* (their son) b. Dec. 2, 1806.

WILLIAM, son of Benjamin and Margaret Bartlett, d. June 25, 1859, æt 33.

Edward W., son of David and Celia Bartlett, d. Oct. 5, 1863, æt 25.

Jeremiah B., son of Alvin and Amey Ann Bartlett, d. Aug. 30, 1872, æt 34.

Levi, son of Benjamin and Margaret Bartlett, d. single, April 13, 1865.

Sylvanus Bartlett, son of Noah, of Smithfield, R. I., m. Sarah Mann, Oct. 10, 1780.

KILLINGLY, CONN., MARRIAGES.

Lettes Bartlett	m.	Sampson B. Covell, Oct. 20, 1831.
Meeora	"	" Elijah Witherby, of Brookfield, March 20, 1837.
Richard	"	" Christina Fisher, April 7, 1831.
Ealezer	"	" Sabina Durfee, Nov. 20, 1830.
Laura	"	" Shubael Day, Sept. 23, 1830.
Waldo	"	" Mary Ann Covell, Sept. 13, 1832.
Israel	"	" Mary Grover of Coventry, Feb. 18, 1821.
John	"	" Patty Bartlett, Nov. 26, 1820.
Mary	"	" Paschael Withey, of Brooklyn, Dec. 28, 1820.
Bethia	"	" Shepard Stearns, Nov. 11, 1827.

PROVIDENCE, R. I. RECORDS.

Moses Bartlett,	m.	Sarah Pool, Aug 18, 1805.
Rosalie	"	" Samuel Drew, Dec. 6, 1815.
Isaac	"	" Lackey Marsh—St. John's Church Records.
		Ext. from Reg. Deeds.]
Josiah	"	of Garland, Me., County of Penobscot.
Reuben	"	" " " "
Joseph	"	" Nottingham, N. H.
Hannah	"	the wife of —— Garland.
Martha	"	" " —— Gruly.
Abigail	"	" " —— Chace.
Sally	"	" " —— Huly.

Deed of land, June 12, 1835, belonging to their father, Nehemiah Bartlett, witnessed by Mercy Bartlett and Ebenezer Bartlett.

Moses H. Bartlett, wife Sarah, a carpenter, owned land on Power street, Providence, R. I.

Joseph Bartlett, of Garland, Me., father, Reuben.

Smith Bartlett, wife, Ann, owned land, 1803. Benefit street, Providence.

OXFORD, MASS.

Levi Bartlett, wife, Eliza, had a son, *Charles Henry*, b. Nov. 12, 1841; d. April 16, 1843.

Betsey Bartlett, m. George Clapp, both of the South Gore, Jan. 1, 1827.

EALEZER BARTLETT, of Fitchburg, and Miram Stowe, of Oxford, m. Jan. 3, 1835.

JAMES O. BARTLETT, a member of the 25th Reg. Mass. Vol. in the Rebellion; d. at Charlestown, Mass., May 1, 1866, of wounds received at Cold Harbor, Va. [Memorial tablet. Town Hall, Oxford, Mass.]

DORCAS BARTLETT, m. Caleb Callum, both of Mendon, Mass., Jan 16, 1791. [*Mendon Records.*]

SARAH BARTLETT, m. Joseph Ballou. b. May 5, 1743, in Wrentham, Mass., May 15, 1766. [*Ballou Genealogy.*]

MARY BARTLETT, b. Jan. 20, 1789; m. Amariah Ballou, in Mt. Desert, Me., Jan. 6, 1825. She was dau. of David Bartlett, of Mt. Desert.

OTHERS OF THE NAME.

The following list of Bartletts who had arrived in this country previous to 1700, all of which are presumed to have emigrated from England, has been obtained from original statistics. Subsequently, there were others who came to these shores. A large field for genealogists is here presented to study the relationship which existed between these early settlers of the Bartlett name who were not associated in emigration to New England.

ROBERT, arrived in Plymouth, Mass., in the ship, Ann, 1623, three years after the landing of the Pilgrims. He d. 1676, aged 73. His descendants are very numerous.

RICHARD, arrived with his family at Newbury, Mass., before 1635. He d. in 1647, æt about 72, and left many descendants. One of his sons, John Bartlett, has been erroneously stated by one writer to be a brother.

JOHN, was in Newport, R. I., and admitted to the town in 1638. He may be the same who was at Windsor, Conn., in 1640.

JOHN, of Windsor, Conn., was there before 1640, and left descendants. He was a brother of George, of Guilford, Conn.

GEORGE, of Guilford, Conn., brother of John, of Windsor, was at Guilford in 1641, and after 1649, of Branford, Conn. He d. in 1669, and left many descendants.

ROBERT, of Hartford, Conn. Said to have been of Cambridge, Mass., in 1632. Was at Hartford, in 1640; removed to Northampton, Mass., in 1665, and was there killed by Indians in 1676. There are many of his descendants.

WILLIAM, of New London, Conn., 1645, was a brother of Robert Bartlett, of the same place. He d. about 1657. No posterity known.

ROBERT, brother of William Bartlett, of New London, Conn., was at that place in 1645, and d. there in 1673. No children known.

NICHOLAS, of Scarborough, Me., and Salem, Mass., was at Scarborough in 1651, and afterward, in 1659, lived in Salem. He was living in 1706, and was then eighty-six years old. He had a wife, Elizabeth, and children.

GEORGE, of Scarborough and Spurwink, Me., 1663, had a dau. who m. Nicholas Baker, of Marblehead, Mass. He may have had other children. He d. about 1674.

ALEXANDER, was probably living at Northampton, Mass., May 27, 1676, as his wife, Sarah, died there at that time.

JOSEPH, of Cambridge and Newton, Mass., was at Cambridge about 1666. He died at Newton in 1702. Many descendants.

BENJAMIN, of Brookfield, Mass., was there before 1700. He had a wife, Mary, and numerous descendants. His daughter, Mary, b. May 6, 1701, was the first birth recorded in the Brookfield records.

JOHN, of Weymouth, Mass., 1666, had a wife, Sarah. He d. in Rehoboth, Mass., Aug. 1684; she died at the same place in Jan., 1684-5. Their descendants are recorded in this book.

ROBERT, of Marblehead, Mass.; was there before 1670, and made a will in 1714. Has descendants. He was b. in Frampton, Dorset County, England, Feb. 4, 1638, and was brother of John, Faithful and Magdaline, all being children of William Bartlett, who died at Frampton, Aug. 26, 1657, and his wife, Edith, who died at the same place, July 10, 1652.

JOHN, of Marblehead, brother of preceding Robert, was born in Frampton, May 14, 1645. In 1711, he states, in an affidavit, that he had lived in Marblehead fifty years. He has descendants.

FAITHFUL, brother of preceding John and Robert, was b. in Frampton, Sept. 18, 1642. He was at Boston, Mass., in 1670, and d. there in 1673. He had a wife, Margret, who administered his estate, and a son, Faithful, b. 1671, and perhaps other children. Magdaline, sister of preceding Faithful, John and Robert, was b. in Frampton in 1629, and lived with her brother's in Marblehead.

DENNIS, was at Marblehead, Mass. His estate was inventoried in 1678. Posterity not traced.

LAURENCE, was in Boston, Mass., in 1670. Posterity not known.

HENRY, was at Marlborough, Mass., in 1680, and has many descendants.

MOSES, d. at Mamamoit, near Plymouth, Mass., 1678. He had a boat which belonged to Joseph Pierce, of Boston, Mass.

JOHN, of Hull, Mass., was there before 1692. He had a wife, Marcy, and numerous descendants.

THOMAS, of Watertown, Mass., 1635, was an original Proprietor of Dedham, Mass. He d. April 26, 1654. In his will he mentions four daughters.

Nearly all of the twenty-three Bartletts enumerated in the preceding list are known to have descendants. That these immigrants, so nearly contemporaneous in their arrival in this country, were connected by consanguity, cannot be doubted, although to this time no effective effort has been made to place them on record in their precise relationship to each other, owing to the magnitude of the work of examining every discernible record touching the history of each. The writer has in his possession a vast amount of matter which has been collected from various reliable sources, relating to all the Bartletts in this country, and it is at the service of any one interested in this line of investigation. As a basis for an enquiry of exceedingly great interest, it is suggested to the student of the name, that an inspection can be made of the popular biographical dictionaries and standard local histories of New England towns.

In the written records and printed histories of many towns, the name frequently appears in creditable connection with public affairs, during the hundred years since the landing of the Pilgrims at Plymouth Rock. From these, it does not appear that the early arrived Bartletts were induced to find homes in the new world, by disappointment in resistance to priestly, and governmental, domination of private right to personal religious belief—so much as by the alluring prospect of founding homes in a land where honorable industry might be better compensated than under the multiform vexations too often prevailing in any country where business and religion are hampered by systems, and procedures, which outlive usefulness and destroy the cheerfulness which should accompany personal enterprise. The Bartletts, like some of the other early settlers who were landed proprietors and owners of estates, were thrifty, forehanded, peacefully inclined persons, who benefit the community of which they are members. Most of them were fairly educated, and it is this love of learning and respect for good order which is significant of a common ancestry. More than one hundred and thirty persons of the name have been graduates of American colleges. The three professions—law, medicine, and divinity—have abundantly demonstrated the fact that the Bartletts have been influential in society as jurisconsults, judges, statesmen, physicians, teachers, and ministers of religion. As generals, and officers high in command in the army and navy, they have been distinguished for courage and bravery.* They have been successful merchants, and have filled with good reputation many positions of public and private trust, and with equal encomium in the more obscure and humble positions in private life, they have been kind neighbors, and steadfast friends, and have adorned their citizenship with integrity and benevolence.

BIOGRAPHICAL.

It was not intended to introduce anything of a general biographical character, but a few abridged extracts from various biographical dictionaries and cyclopædias with reference to some of the more prominent of the Bartletts, selected, as nearly as practicable, from the descendants of each of those who, as progenitors of the name, first settled in this country, may not be unacceptable.

JOSIAH BARTLETT, who was distinguished by being one of the signers of the Declaration of Independence, died in the 66th year of his age, after a noble life spent in the service of his fellow-men. He was a physician, with a large practice, in New Hampshire, and his political career commenced in 1765, when he was chosen Representative for Kingston in the Legislature of what was then the province. In 1775, he was chosen a delegate to the Continental Congress, and went to Philadelphia. There, in July, 1776, Congress concluded to vote upon the adoption of that instrument which made the people forever free. Josiah Bartlett, of New Hampshire, was the first called who answered in the affirmative, at the roll-call by States. He was the first man, after the President, who put his name to the paper. In 1776, after laborious work for his country as member of the Congress, he was active in the military business of New Hampshire. He

* "The Official Register of Volunteer force of the U. S. Army, 1861-65," contains the names of eighty-six Bartletts who were commissioned officers in the army during the late War of the Rebellion. It was not ascertained how many were officers in the navy during that period, but it is presumed there was a proportionate number.

was Chief Justice of the Court of Common Pleas, in 1780, and Muster Master in raising troops. In 1788, he was Chief Justice of the Supreme Court. In 1787, he was an active member of the convention held in New York, to devise a plan for the government of the Confederation of States. He was Chief Magistrate when New Hampshire adopted a temporary constitution, in 1776, and Governor of the State, 1792-93. He was also a presidential elector. His three sons were all eminent physicians, and his six daughters were admirable children of their worthy sire.

WILLIAM FRANCIS BARTLETT, son of Charles L., a Boston merchant, was the youngest major-general in the service of his country during the war for the Union. His biography can be found in almost any public library. He was a Harvard student, and in his junior term relinquished his studies to enter himself as a soldier for the war, he being then twenty-two years old. While convalescing after losing a leg in the line of duty, he returned to Harvard to take his university degree, in 1862. His promotion by President Lincoln to be brigadier general, for bravery, was followed by his brevet as major-general. His life reads like a romance of heroism and nobility. He married, Oct., 1865, Agnes, daughter of Seth Pomeroy, of Pittsfield, Mass, a great grand-daughter of Seth Pomeroy, of the Revolutionary War. He resigned his commission in 1866, and, after a visit to Europe, settled in Pittsfield, Mass., and was the manager of the West Stockbridge, Mass., iron works, and also of iron works at Richmond, Va. The Alumni Association of Harvard University met after his death and took measures for procuring the memorial in marble which is placed in Memorial Hall, in that institution of learning. He left three sons and three daughters. Among the many tributes to the memory of this heroic patriot soldier, are two poems, one by Bret Harte, the other by John Greenleaf Whittier.

The following is copied from a page in *Scribner's Magazine*, August, 1878:

"*Palfrey's Memoir of William Francis Bartlett*"

"What is the use, it may be asked, of writing novels and inventing verses while the human race has vitality enough to produce such men as

General Bartlett? A Harvard undergraduate, who steps into the ranks a mere boy and rises by bravery and merit from private in a militia regiment to brevet major-general in the army, during a four year's war, at the close of which, he is but reaching his twenty-fifth birthday, is a sufficiently striking figure. But when one reads the story of this stripling officer, how he never lost presence of mind or ready wisdom of decision in such awful carnage as that at Ball's Bluff and Port Hudson, and how he bore the torture of wounds and the torment of cruel captivity, how he had a leg crushed by a minie-ball, in the Peninsula, how he was wounded in the head, badly wounded in the hand, hurt in his remaining leg, had his wooden leg crushed in the crater at Petersburg, and how in spite of all, he held the shattered remains of his body to hard and perilous duty, one gains an unwonted faith in human nature, and a higher ideal of manhood. He was never bitter toward his foes; indeed, he was one of the first to appreciate their courage and sincerity, and at the centennial anniversary of the battle of Lexington, made a short speech, full of irresistible fire and persuasiveness, urging a conciliatory policy toward the South. He knew how to refuse a large legacy from generous motives, and when one party wanted him to run for lieutenant-governor, and the dominant party would have given him the governorship, he refused both on some scruple of honor, though the panic had made him poor and thrown him out of business.

"Whittier has made Bartlett the subject of one of his finest poems, and Bret Hart sang his requiem in these pages, but when one has read the little volume that reveals the inner and outer life of the man, written poems seem feeble and adjectives grow weak. If any man falls into skepticism about the country through manifold temptation of New York Tweeds, and South Carolina carpet-baggers, let him read this life and find his faith refreshed. Such a man makes the earth wholesome."

WASHINGTON BARTLETT, was born in Savannah, Ga., in 1824; died in Oakland, Cal., Sept. 12, 1887. He removed to California in 1850, settling in San Francisco, where he published the first daily newspaper issued in that city. In 1859, he was elected county clerk. In 1870, appointed harbor commissioner. In 1882 and 1884, was elected Mayor of San Francisco; and in 1886, elected Governor of the State, holding the latter office at the time of his death.

THOMAS BARTLETT, who died in 1805, was a lieutenant-colonel under General Stark, and was at the surrender of Burgoyne. He was in command of a regiment at West Point, at the time of Benedict Arnold's acts of treason, and was Speaker of the New Hampshire House of Representatives. He was also a judge.

JOHN R. BARTLETT, was born Sept. 26, 1843. He was appointed to the Naval Academy from Rhode Island in 1859, and, in 1861, was on the steamship Mississippi, which passed Forts Jackson and Phillips, at the capture of New Orleans. He was made ensign in 1863, lieutenant in 1864, and was in the steam sloop, Susquehanna, in both attacks upon Fort Fisher, and was one of the assaulting party at its capture by Admiral Porter and General Alfred H. Terry, and was particularly mentioned for his bravery by Commodore Gordon and Commander Blake. He was Lieutenant Commander at the Naval Academy in 1867–69, and Commander in 1887, and afterwards on duty at the Naval Department in Washington, D. C., as Hydrographer.

BAILEY BARTLETT, born in Haverhill, in 1750. He was a member at different times of both branches of the Massachusetts Legislature, and member of the state convention which adopted the Constitution of the United States ; member of Congress, from 1797, four years, and died in 1830. He was a personal friend and associate of John and Samuel Adams.

ICHABOD BARTLETT, was a celebrated lawyer. He was born in Salisbury, N. H., July 24, 1786, and died at Portsmouth, N. H., Oct. 19, 1853. Graduate of Dartmouth College in 1808. Admitted to the bar in 1811. He removed to Portsmouth in 1816, where he achieved high rank in his profession, having as competitors Daniel Webster and Mason. He was an officer of the state militia, was seven times elected to the Legislature, and was speaker of the House in 1821, Clerk of the State Senate in 1817–18, Solicitor of Rockingham County in 1819–21, elected to Congress in 1823, twice re-elected, serving until March, 1829. He held other honorable positions, declining the proffer of the Chief Justiceship of the state.

ENOCH BARTLETT, who died in 1860, was born in Haverhill in 1779. He was a merchant in the truest meaning of the word, and was an extensive importer of foreign mer-

chandise, during the troublous 1812 period, when merchants
suffered heavy losses by the depredations of the enemy on
the seas. He it was, after whom the favorite Bartlett pear
was named.

EDWIN BARTLETT, of Annandale, N. Y., was engaged
in commercial pursuits in the South American States and was
Consul at Lima, Peru. He traveled in many foreign coun-
tries, and established his homestead near Tarrytown, N. Y.,
naming the place Rockwood. He was one of the six men
who originated, organized and founded the Pacific Mail Steamship Company, and was one of the incorporators of the
Panama Railroad Company.

JOHN RUSSELL BARTLETT, born in Providence,
R. I., Oct. 23, 1805, and died there, May 28, 1886. He was
educated for mercantile pursuits. For six years was cashier
of the Globe Bank, Providence. Was one of the founders of
the Providence Athenæum, and member of the Franklin
Society. He was in the book importing business in New
York in 1837, the firm name being Bartlett & Welford. Was
a member of the American Ethnological Society, and Corresponding Secretary of the New York Historical Society.
He was also an honorary member of many of the learned
societies of Europe and America. He was appointed by
President Zachary Taylor to fix the boundary line between
theUnited States and Mexico, and while in this service made
extensive explorations. On his return, he published a personal narrative of the places visited. He was delegated by
several learned societies to represent them at the Interna-
tional Congress of Archæology at Antwerp, and the Congress
of Anthropology and Prehistoric Archæology at Paris. He
was one of the United States Commissioners to the Interna-
tional Prison Congress at London. In both Europe and
America, he was especially distinguished in archæology, phi-
lology, bibliography, and as an author of authoritative scientific and literary works, of which he published a large number. He was for seventeen years Secretary of State of
Rhode Island, from 1855 to 1872.

WILLIAM HOLMES CHAMBERS BARTLETT, born in Lancaster, Penn., in 1804. Appointed from Missouri to United Sates Military Academy, at West Point. Graduated in 1826 at the head of his class. Professor of engineering and other branches at the Military Academy, was A. M., by New Jersey College at Princeton, N. J., in 1837 ; L. L. D., by Geneva College, N. Y., in 1847. He retired from active service in 1871, with the rank of Colonel. He was the author of many scientific works and a member of different learned societies.

WILLIAM PITT GREENWOOD BARTLETT, was born in Boston, in 1837. Graduated at Harvard in 1858 ; was an accomplished mathematician when a young man. He was proctor of college in 1859-1862, was one of the corps of computors for the *Nautical Almanac*, and a writer upon scientific topics. He died in 1865, at Cambridge, Mass.

WILLIAM BARTLETT, one of the founders of Andover Theological Seminary, born in Newburyport in 1748. He was engaged in mercantile enterprises, and, acquiring great wealth, used his means liberally in advancing the cause of religion, assisting the needy, and in the furtherance of various benevolent and philanthropic projects. It is estimated that his benefactions amounted to over half a million dollars, of which the Andover Theological Seminary received $250,000.

WILLIAM C. BARTLETT, born in New York. Graduated at the U. S. Military Academy at West Point in 1862, as 2d lieutenant ; breveted 1st lieutenant Sept. 17, 1862, for gallant and meritorious services at the battle of Antietam ; breveted captain, Nov. 16, 1863, for bravery at Cambell's Station, Tenn.; captain staff, March 19, 1864 ; breveted major, Sept. 1. 1864, for gallant and meritorious services during the Atlanta campaign ; breveted brigadier general, March 13, 1865. He was in many engagements during the war and his successive promotions were for bravery and meritorious services.

JOSIAH BARTLETT, son of George Bartlett, of Charlestown, Mass., was born there in 1759. He studied medicine,

and practiced as surgeon in ships of war and in Charlestown.
He was elected to the Massachusetts Legislature as senator,
and also as representative ; was a member of the Governor's
Council ; was Grand Master of the Grand Lodge of Free-
masons ; delivered many orations, and published many books
upon miscellaneous subjects. He died March 5, 1820.

THOMAS BARTLETT, Jr., born in Vermont. He was
a lawyer. Was county attorney, 1839-41. President of the
Vermont Constitutional Convention of 1850. Was elected
to the Vermont Legislature, and served in both houses. Was
elected to Congress, and served as representative, 1851-53.

ELISHA BARTLETT, born in Smithfield, R. I., in 1804,
and died there in 1855. Graduated at Brown University
in 1826. He practiced medicine in Lowell and Worcester,
Mass. Was Mayor of Lowell. Filled the chair of medicine
at Dartmouth College, Transylvania College, Lexington, Ky.,
University of Maryland, University of New York, Vermont
Medical College, and the chair of Materia Medica and juris-
prudence, at the College of Physicians and Surgeons, New
York. He was author of many valuable medical works,
and achieved distinction as author and physician.

SAMUEL COLCORD BARTLETT, a professor of sacred
theology at the Chicago Theological Seminary, and a professor
of intellectual philosophy and rhetoric, at Western Reserve
College, Ohio. He was a pastor of the New England Church,
at Chicago, Ill., and also pastor of the Congregational Church,
at Monson, Mass.

JOSEPH BARTLETT, born at Plymouth, Mass., in 1763,
had a life of adventure. Graduated at Harvard in 1782. He
was of an erratic fancy, and although gifted with phenomenal
talent, he may be said to have been a splendid failure. Play-
wright, poet, lawyer, orator on occasions, a free-thinker, a
captain in Shay's rebellion, a representative in the Maine
Legislature, and nearly elected to Congress, only lacking
a few votes. In London, he was an actor, and afterwards a
merchant and suffered shipwreck on Cape Cod, having sailed

for these shores with a cargo of merchandise obtained on
credit in England. In 1799, he delivered a poem at Cambridge, before the Phi Beta Society, and produced various
desultory writings, which gave evidence of a strong satirical
faculty. He died in 1827.

WASHINGTON ALLEN BARTLETT, born in 1820;
died in 1871. Was Alcalde at San Francisco in 1846. He
had been a lieutenant in an American vessel and was selected
for the position on account of his knowledge of the Spanish
language. He afterwards served in the U. S. navy. His
daughter, Frances Aurelia, married Sig. Orviedo, a rich Cuban.
A poem, written by Stedman, entitled, the " Diamond Wedding," appeared after the marriage ceremonies and attracted
great attention in society. Sig. Orviedo died in a few years
after their marriage, and his widow, Frances Aurelia, then
became the Countess Von Glumer, having married Count
Von Glumer, a gentleman well known in Mexican military
circles. They reside in the City of Mexico.

HENRY A. BARTLETT, born in Rhode Island, a son of
John R. Bartlett, and was appointed Lieutenant of the Marine
Corps, Oct. 16, 1861 ; Captain, Nov. 29, 1867. From July,
1862 to Aug, 1864, he served in the iron-clad " New Ironsides," during the numerous engagements with the forts and
batteries of Charlestown harbor.

WILLIAM LEHMAN ASHMEAD BARTLETT, a descendant from the Plymouth Bartletts, is prominent as a private secretary and almoner for Baroness Burdett-Coutts,
whose husband he became Feb. 12, 1881. He was son of
Ellis Bartlett, an American merchant, and was born at New
Brunswick, N. J., in 1851. He went to England, 1861. Was
educated at Uppingham School and Keble College, Oxford,
where he held a scholarship. He graduated at Christ Church,
and studied law. He was private secretary for the Baroness,
during the Russian War, 1877-78, and her almoner in connection with the Turkish Compassionate Fund, and took a
part in journalism. He published a book on the Turko-
Russian War. In 1886, was elected to Parliament and was

re-elected by an increased majority. By Royal license, he assumed the name, "Burdett-Coutts." His brother, Ellis Ashmead Bartlett, was born in Philadelphia, Penn.; graduated at Christ Church College, Oxford, England, and distinguished himself as a scholar. He became a member of parliament and was appointed to office in the Admiralty.

TRUMAN H. BARTLETT is the widely known sculptor. A description of his studio in Boston was published in the *Sunday Herald*, of that city, May 8, 1880, the article giving some account of the career of this famous artist. He was born in Dorset, Vermont, Oct. 25, 1836. He worked in boyhood under the tuition of Robert E. Launitz, of New York. His first bust in marble was made in Waterbury, Conn., in 1863. He also made busts of some of the prominent men of New Haven, and Hartford, of the same State, and being assisted by a wealthy merchant of Hartford, David H. Clark, he went to Rome, and thence to Paris, doing monumental work. His statue of Horace Wells, the discoverer of the anæsthetic properties of nitrous-oxide gas, is placed on the capitol grounds at Hartford. He has designed some of the noblest monuments in the country. He has a son, Paul, who bids fair to make a reputation as a sculptor equal to that of his father.

JOSEPH J. BARTLETT, was born in 1820, was appointed Brigadier General, Oct., 1862, and promoted to brevet Major General in 1864. From 1867 to 1869, he was United States Minister to Sweden and Norway, and recently an officer in the Pension Bureau at Washington, D. C.

JOHN BARTLETT. There was a John Bartlett, born in the 16th century, in England, eminent as a musician. He published a book of "Ayres, with a triplicate of Musicke, whereof the First is for the Lute or Opharion and Viole de Gamba, and 4 Parts to Sing. The Second Part is for 2 Trebles to sing to the Lute and Viola. The Third Part is for the Lute and one Voyce, and the Viola de Gamba." The work was published by John Mullet in 1606, and was dedicated to " the Right Honourable, My singular good Lord and Maister, Sir Edward Seymore." The author took the degree, B. M., at Oxford in 1610.

WILLIAM HENRY BARTLETT, author and artist, born at Kentish Town, London, 1809. Many of the finest drawings in *Brittons Cathedral Antiquities of England*, were executed by him. In 1832, in conjuction with Dr. Beattie, he published an illustrated work in Switzerland. This was followed by a large number of similar works. The number of plates they contain, engraved from his drawings, is nearly a thousand. He visited this country four times between 1834 and 1853. In 1844, appeared his *Walks About Jerusalem*, the precursor of a number of works illustrating the Orient. He undertook a sixth journey to the east in 1855, to study the Seven Churches of Asia Minor, and, escaping the dangers of pestilence and robbery, was successful. He died on his passage homeward from Malta. His labors resulted in the posthumous publication, *Jerusalem Revisited*. He was amiable, generous, instructive as a writer, and an artist of great ability.

RICHARD BARTLETT, born in England in 1469, and died in 1556. Was educated at All Souls' College, Oxford. He studied medicine, and was a physician of great eminence. Was President of the College of Physicians. [*Cooper's Biog. Dictionary.*]

REMINISCENCES.

The occasion for a gathering of notable men in Boston, in 1879, was a dinner given to Hon. Sidney Bartlett, by Hon. John B. Alley, of Massachusetts, when were present Vice-President Wheeler, Chief Justice Wait, Secretary Evarts, Senator Dawes, and other gentlemen distinguished in governmental life. Hon. Sidney Bartlett was probably as profound a student of the Constitution of the United States as any lawyer in the country. As counsellor in great enter-

prises, he had no equal in influence or knowledge of legal
principles, and his work in connection with the most important railroad projects, and the like, was greatly appreciated by
the leading men of different parts of the country.   As a lawyer, he made no errors, and his great capacity and forecast
gave to his opinions a character which was never distrusted.

The unveiling of the statue erected at Amesbury, Mass., in
honor of Governor Josiah Bartlett, will long be remembered
by thousands of people who participated in the ceremonial,
July 4, 1888. The newspapers of the country published
accounts of the proceedings at that time.   The statue was a
gift to the state of Massachusetts, from Jacob R. Huntington.
There was a large parade of military and civic bodies, the
Lieutenant Governor and Legislature being guests of the
town.

The statue was unveiled by John S. Poyen, Jr., a lineal descendant of Josiah Bartlett.   As a part of the exercises, a poem
by Whittier was read, in which is the quatrain :

> " Amid those picked and chosen men,
>   Than his, who here first drew his breath,
> No firmer fingers held the pen,
>   That wrote for liberty or death."

There is a murial tablet in the Park Congregational Church,
at Norwich, Conn., to the memory of Prof. D. E. Bartlett.   It
is of white marble and bears this inscription : "The deaf
mutes' memorial of their friend and teacher in the gospel,
David Ely Bartlett, born Sept. 29, 1805 ; died Nov. 29, 1879.
The ears of the deaf shall be unstopped and the tongue of the
dumb shall sing."   The ceremonies at the memorial services
were of great interest, a hundred and twenty-five deaf mutes
taking part. Rev. L. W. Bacon preached a scholarly discourse
on the occasion, which was interpreted for the deaf mutes by
Prof. Abel S. Clark, of the American Institute, Boston, Mass.

CONCLUSION.

Many women born to the Bartlett name, have had their full share of the love and respect of the communities in which they have lived. To them, must loyal honors be paid for the great part they have performed as partners in the founding of families and establishing happy, well-ordered homes. Their descendants are the most worthy citizens of this republic, and to their influence is doubtless due the fact that rarely has the name of Bartlett been mentioned in connection with anything of an unfortunate nature. Eliza Bartlett was an exemplar of the spirit which actuated the women of New England in the days of our forefathers. She, with her young son, sailed, in 1712, from England in the ship Mary, for a Massachusetts port. A voyage of such length in those days was not without such hardships and peril as daunt any but a resolute person, but the early history of New England gives evidence of the self-sacrifice and heroism of women of the Bartlett name, not more nor less noteworthy than that exhibited in the adventure of Eliza Bartlett.

At the family reunions, whenever they have been held at any place, the Bartletts have assembled from all parts of the United States, and these assemblages have been of great interest to all who love the history of this country. Old traditions of the origin of the race are rehearsed, but recently there has been no going further into the subject than that in connection with the first of the name who came into England from Normandy. This little book, will, it is thought, correct some errors which, arising from conjecture, have obtained some credence.

INDEX TO CHRISTIAN NAMES.

INDEX TO SURNAMES

www.ingramcontent.com/pod-product-compliance
Lightning Source LLC
Chambersburg PA
CBHW020801020726
47495CB00008B/2541

* 9 7 8 3 3 3 7 0 7 4 7 6 0 *